"We can't go back and undo it, no matter how badly we may want to."

"I, um... Yeah." Rick stumbled over his words. What could he say?

"And I know we can't totally act as if it never happened," Becca said.

That was certain. Rick knew he would never, *ever* forget those moments Becca had held him as if he were the center of her universe. "No, probably not."

"But I need to ask a favor."

"Anything."

"It would hurt innocent people if this got out. My children, my in-laws. They might think it was some reflection of my feelings for Gabe. I loved my husband with my whole heart. Please don't tell anyone what happened." Her voice was husky, reminding him of the way she'd murmured in his ear as she'd made love to him. Even then, he'd understood that Becca was Gabe's forever. What Rick had experienced with her had been an aberration.

An intense aberration he couldn't quite get off his mind.

Dear Reader,

When I wrote Royce McIntyre's story in *Temporary Nanny,* I instantly knew that his sister Becca would have her own book. Some characters simply grab my attention, and that's exactly what Becca did. She was a fully developed person from the start, even for her small appearance in Royce's story.

The idea for *Baby, I'm Yours* crystallized after my editor approached me about writing a book for a special baby-theme month. I knew I wanted Becca to be the heroine, but there were certain areas of her personal life that would need to be modified (I'm purposely being vague so I don't let slip any spoilers).

I loved Becca's abundant, chaotic life, complete with a full-time job, three children and in-laws who lived in her basement. Her plate was so full I was hesitant to add more complications. But add them I did.

I hope you will find the result a delicious set of circumstances. Delicious in that Becca and Rick are challenged to their cores and must dig deep within themselves to find the courage to love again.

If their story strikes a chord in you, please feel free to drop me an e-mail at CarrieAuthor@aol.com. I can also receive letters at P.O. Box 6045, Chandler, AZ 85246-6045. I love hearing from my readers!

Warm wishes,

Carrie Weaver

BABY, I'M YOURS
Carrie Weaver

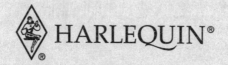

TORONTO • NEW YORK • LONDON
AMSTERDAM • PARIS • SYDNEY • HAMBURG
STOCKHOLM • ATHENS • TOKYO • MILAN • MADRID
PRAGUE • WARSAW • BUDAPEST • AUCKLAND

ISBN-13: 978-0-373-78221-5
ISBN-10:   0-373-78221-7

BABY, I'M YOURS

Printed in U.S.A.

ABOUT THE AUTHOR

Best parenting advice ever received? Even if your children aren't listening to a word you say, keep communicating. We often don't know what sinks in until our children are adults. **Favorite bedtime story?** As a child, my favorite bedtime book was *The Sleepy Puppy*. I can still remember the refrain, "Puppies need lots of sleep and lots of love." A pretty good lesson to live by. I continued the tradition of reading at bedtime with my own two sons. **Favorite quote from your mom?** My mom taught me more by her actions than her words. By observing her selflessness, I learned how to love unconditionally, to give my all without wondering what I'll receive in return. **If you could've kept your child at a specific age, what would that be?** In utero. No colic, no temper tantrums, no wondering where they are at 2:00 a.m. ;-) **Most poignant moment with your own bundle of joy?** My most poignant moment was the first time my infant son smiled when I entered a room and I realized he wasn't gassy; I was simply the center of his universe. What an awesome gift. What an awesome re-sponsibility. **What makes a mom?** Love… sacrifice…love…patience…love…dedication…love… You can see where I'm going with this.

Books by Carrie Weaver

HARLEQUIN SUPERROMANCE

HARLEQUIN NASCAR

This book is for Sandy Zipp, my friend
and fellow single mom in the trenches

PROLOGUE

BECCA SMITH STRETCHED, shielding her eyes from the sun. This was the absolute best day ever. But then again, she'd thought the same thing yesterday at Walt Disney World. And the day before that. And pretty much every day for the past twenty years.

She glanced sideways at Gabe, lying prone on a deck chair next to her. He was every bit as handsome as the first day she'd seen him in seventh-grade science class. Maybe even more so. After all these years, she still couldn't help smiling when he entered a room. Except, of course, on the very rare occasions when they argued.

As if sensing her appraisal, Gabe opened one eye and grinned. "You look very content."

"I am. I liked Walt Disney World, but I could get addicted to cruising the Caribbean. There's nothing we have to do, except nap and work on our tans. And I love having you all to myself."

He reached over and grasped her hand, rubbing her knuckles with his thumb in that slow, sexy way that thrilled her. "I like knowing we can make love whenever we want, day or night, without worrying about being interrupted. No kids, no parents, no pets. Just me and you, naked in our cabin, with all the time in the world. That way I can devote the kind of attention to you that you deserve, from head to toe."

Becca fanned herself with her paperback novel, recalling the way he'd made love with her this morning. Slow, delicious caresses combined with an inventive position that had left her feeling young, sated and absolutely desirable.

She turned toward him, resting her head against her arm, trying not to wish every single day could be like this. "It has been a special trip. I feel like we've recaptured parts of our relationship that sometimes get lost in the everyday hassles."

"Yeah. It seems we're both going in so many directions, there isn't time left for us to just relax together." He scanned the horizon for a moment, then his gaze met hers, honest and intimate. His voice was husky when he said, "I've missed that."

His admission touched Becca. It reminded her that her big, strong, heroic husband had vulnerabilities, too. Smiling, she traced his biceps with her finger. "Me, too. Only I didn't realize how much I missed it until this vacation…. Let's not allow another twenty years go by before we do this again—simply be Becca and Gabe, a couple in love."

"I haven't done such a good job of making that a priority, have I?"

"We both get caught up in our jobs, the kids, your parents. It just sneaks up on us. But maybe we can make a conscious effort not to let it happen again. We can schedule dates, get away for more weekends alone."

Gabe leaned close, cupping her neck with his hand and kissing her. "You are absolutely my top priority, lady, and I intend to show you that every single day."

"Oh, Gabe, you already do. The little surprises you plan for me, the phone calls every day. I feel guilty for even wanting more." Becca smiled, caressing his jaw. "It's been a glorious adventure. One I wouldn't have missed for anything. We have three beautiful children and a wonderful life."

"And it's just going to keep getting better."

"Absolutely. Except…one thing."

Frowning, he raised his head. "What's wrong?"

"We've only got two more days and then it's back to reality. I think there are other ways I'd rather spend this afternoon than working on my tan."

"Oh?" Gabe's grin was wicked. His gaze traveled over her, making her glad she'd splurged on a bikini for the trip and put in extra time on her treadmill.

"I bought a set of Kama Sutra cards in the gift shop I'm just dying to open."

He stood and held out his hand to her. "Have I told you recently how much I love you?"

Becca placed her hand in his and stood, so close she could see the black ringing his brown irises. Her heart constricted at the intensity of his gaze. This gorgeous, kind, wonderful man wanted her, now and forever. It never ceased to amaze her. "Not in the past hour or so."

"I love you, Bec." Gabe kissed her deeply, each stroke of his tongue a promise. "Always," he murmured against her mouth.

Becca twined her arms around his neck and responded eagerly, feeling almost a teen again. Only now, the passion was tempered with years of friendship, shared dreams and goals.

"I love you, Gabe. Always."

CHAPTER ONE

Three Years Later

BECCA SMITH SQUEEZED her eyes shut and waited for the dizziness to pass. And hoped this horrible day was nearly over.

"Are you okay?"

She opened her eyes to see Rick Jensen's concerned gaze. During the funeral, the presence of her husband's best friend and business partner had had a calming effect on her.

But now, Becca longed to scream and keep on screaming, until everyone quit tiptoeing around the fact that Gabe was dead and her life would never be "okay" again. Then she was sure the muted conversations around her would end and her friends and family would scuttle back to their unscathed lives. Their new year would soon return to normal.

The urge to throw casserole dishes and rented glassware against the wall was almost overwhelming, as if the shards raining down on the tile floor could convey how brittle and broken she felt.

But Becca held it together long enough to nod. Somehow, she would make it through the wake.

"Have you eaten today?"

"I—I think so." It was a lie. But she knew Rick would never understand that her throat constricted every time she took a bite.

He touched her arm. "How about if I fix you a plate? You look like you're ready to drop."

"That would be…nice." She understood his need to make things better for her, knew that her grief reminded him of his own loss—the two men had been as close as brothers. And she wished with her whole heart that food was the answer. But it wasn't.

When Rick handed her a heaping plate a couple of minutes later, Becca fought a wave of nausea. But she obediently pushed the food around with her fork.

"You've got to eat something. For them." Rick nodded toward her three children: sixteen-year-old Maya, ten-year-old Aaron and their brother, David, now twenty. The three stood huddled together on one side of the living room.

It was as if they realized how vulnerable they

were without their strong father standing between them and the world. Or maybe they suspected their normally patient mother was one scream away from losing it in front of all these well-meaning people.

"How much longer?" she asked.

"How much longer for what?"

"Until they leave." Until she could be alone with her grief and not pretend to be in control. Until she could surrender to the hopelessness threatening to incapacitate her.

"Pretty soon. Why don't you go upstairs and lie down. I can let Gabe's folks know. And I'm sure Royce and Katy wouldn't mind taking over host duties."

"No, I need to do it. For Gabe."

Emotion flashed in his eyes, then was gone. "Okay."

Becca was barely aware when he moved away from her. Or when he spoke quietly to her brother, Royce, and they worked the room in tandem.

All she knew was that people streamed over to say a quick goodbye at precise intervals.

Becca hoped she would remember to thank Rick for his kindness. But the task of staying focused on her hostess duties was almost more than she could handle.

When the last guest left, she closed the door, leaning her forehead against it.

Then was pulled into a strong embrace.

Gabe.

But it wasn't his scent. It was her brother's.

Becca stiffened, wondering how she could have confused a brotherly embrace with that of her soul mate. Then she forgave herself for the silly slip, stepping into his arms and hiding as if she were a girl of five again.

"I'm so sorry. I should have seen you weren't holding up as well as you wanted us to believe," Royce said.

"I'm fine."

"No, you're not." He drew back and held her gaze. Touching her cheek, he asked, "Have you cried?"

"No. I can't. My husband is…dead…and I can't seem to cry. I'm just so darn angry."

"Maybe you could use some time alone. Katy and I are going to take Dad and Evelyn to the airport in a few minutes. How about if David, Maya and Aaron come with us to see them off? Then on our way home, we'll take the kids to the movies—give everyone a little reprieve."

"I don't suppose Jim and Irene would want to go?" Becca felt guilty even as she asked the question, putting her need to be alone above her in-laws' grief.

"We asked Gabe's folks to come, but they said they want some quiet time alone at the cemetery to say goodbye to Gabe."

"Thank you." She hoped those two words adequately expressed her gratitude for what amounted to a lifeline.

Her feelings must have shown, because Royce said, "That way you can have some alone time yourself and let go. Quit being brave."

"I'm not brave. I'm…sad and confused and so totally p.o.'d, I can barely see straight."

"That's understandable."

Her sister-in-law, Katy, approached. "Everyone's on board for the airport, then the movies." She turned to Becca and gave her a quick hug. "We'll clean up when we get home. You don't do a thing, except maybe take a long, hot bath and crawl into bed."

"Thank you." If the circumstances had been different, Becca would have loved to join them. But as it was, she was just too damn grateful for a few moments of solitude.

Rick came up beside her and touched her arm. "You need anything, *anything,* call me."

"Thank you."

She hugged her kids, her in-laws and her parents and finally they all left.

For possibly the first time in twenty-three years, Becca was totally alone.

She started up the stairs to take a bath, but stopped halfway. She simply couldn't face the master bedroom and bath, where every corner, every cubic inch of air, reflected her life with Gabe. Her first love. Her *only* love.

Instead, she retraced her steps to the great room, automatically picking up plates and glassware. By rote, she cleared the room, twining her fingers through several glasses.

One was slick and she started to lose her grip as she walked into the kitchen.

Though she tried to save it, the glass fell to the tiled floor and shattered.

Just as Becca's life had slipped out of control and broken to bits.

Powerful emotions bubbled within her, emotions foreign yet somehow right. Red-hot rage. Rage at Gabe for promising her forever and staying only twenty-three years. And anger at a God who had taken him away.

The sound of glass shattering was the perfect accompaniment to her anger. She grabbed glass after rented glass and dashed it to the floor, glorying in the power of defiance.

Becca had always played by the rules. She'd been a loving wife, a good mother. She'd treated her in-laws with kindness. Worked hard, volunteered her time, attended church. She had done everything she was supposed to do and her family should have been protected from bad things.

But fate hadn't played by the rules. It had delivered a massive heart attack to an otherwise healthy husband and father.

RICK LEANED his forehead against the cold steering wheel, his breath condensing as he exhaled. He should go home, get out of the Smith driveway. But he couldn't seem to turn the key in the ignition. Because once he did, Gabe's life would be past tense. The funeral was over, the wake was over, and now life was supposed to go on as usual.

But life as usual was no longer possible. Because Gabe wouldn't be in the office to help build up their rental-car business, playing off Rick's strengths and weaknesses. There wouldn't be anybody to clap him on the shoulder after a hard day and suggest stopping for a beer. And there sure wouldn't be anyone close enough to know what he'd gone through during his divorce, except maybe Becca.

Rick suspected he would never be the same again. He couldn't just sail through life, taking for granted that he had decades of good health ahead of him. Not only had he suddenly lost his best friend, he'd also come face-to-face with his own mortality. And he didn't much like it. If a guy as vital as Gabe could be struck down by a heart attack, then it could happen to anyone.

He straightened, staring at the house as if to find answers. Maybe even hoping Gabe would come strolling out the door saying it was all a huge joke. Rick would give everything he had to make that happen. But he couldn't.

Glancing at the passenger seat, he eyed the files Becca had requested. He should leave them for another day, but she had been insistent. Becca was a hairdresser, but also worked for Reliable Car Rental as their part-time accounts-receivable clerk. She knew as well as he did that the business needed to keep the cash flowing.

But there was no way in hell he wanted to go back into that house today. No way he wanted to look into Becca's eyes and see blank despair. Her stoic refusal to grieve had touched him more than a flood of tears. She was hurting, no doubt about it. And seeing her so lost and alone threatened his own tentative composure.

Nodding, Rick started the engine, flicked on the heater and put the gearshift in Reverse.

But he couldn't seem to let his foot off the brake.

Becca needed him.

BECCA WAS BARELY aware of the tears streaming down her face. Or of the glass stinging her calves, leaving pinpricks of blood on her skin.

The only thing she knew was that something immobilized her right arm.

Trying to wrench away, she swung, ready to do battle with whoever stood between her and her mission.

Rick's hand tightened on her wrist. "No, Becca."

"Let me go." She watched in horror as the palm of her left hand connected with his cheek. Felt the sting of flesh meeting flesh. And knew she'd never forgive herself, even if Rick did. But something propelled her movements, something she didn't understand.

He grasped both wrists. "Calm down."

"I don't want to calm down."

Removing the tumbler from her hand, he set it on the counter.

Becca's fingers flexed as she glanced longingly at the glass. Destruction felt like the perfect response to destruction. And soothed her in a way nothing else had.

Nodding, she pretended to acquiesce, employing as much cunning as an alcoholic seeking a drink.

Rick pulled her into his arms, murmuring soothing words.

She allowed herself to relax for a moment. Rest her cheek against his gabardine jacket. He was a good friend and only meant to comfort. But he just didn't understand. He'd lost a friend, but she'd lost the center of her life.

Becca felt as if she was spinning out of control with nothing to anchor her. Except, perhaps, the sound of glass shattering on tile.

Reaching blindly, she patted the counter until she felt something smooth and cylindrical.

"Enough, Becca."

She struggled, fighting for her life. Or maybe fighting for Gabe's life. It was all such a confusing mess.

Rick reached for her wrist again.

Becca evaded his grasp, shoving him with her shoulder.

He lost his balance and started to fall backward, pulling her with him.

Grunting as he hit the floor, Rick cushioned her fall.

Becca tried to scramble to her feet, but he held her fast, his arm pinning her against him.

"No, Becca. No more."

She had lost the battle. Her ragged breathing slowed as the fight went out of her. Replaced by deep, wracking sobs. All her hurt and despair came pouring out.

Barely aware of Rick patting her back, murmuring soothing words, she lost herself in a rush of release at no longer having to pretend she could go on without Gabe.

Cradled by Rick, she curled into the fetal position and cried out her sorrow. Emotion rocked her body with the rhythm of her sobs.

Rick's chest heaved, as if her sorrow was too much for him. Or as if her loss of control had touched off an explosion of grief in him.

Glancing up at his face, Becca touched his wet cheeks. She shouldn't have been surprised. He loved Gabe nearly as much as she did.

And that knowledge calmed her, much to her surprise.

Still, Rick held her, murmuring encouragement.

After what seemed like hours, awareness seeped in. Primal awareness.

Movement, friction, two bodies in such proximity had mimicked a coupling so unlikely it was laughable. If she'd had an ounce of her sense of humor left.

Becca glanced up, holding Rick's startled gaze.

"I'm sorry, Bec. It's one of those automatic responses." He set her aside, his husky use of her nickname touching off memories of the many times Gabe had whispered the same in the dark.

If she closed her eyes, she could almost pretend he was Gabe. Pretend it was her mate's body that responded to hers. And suddenly, she wanted one last opportunity to be with Gabe. To pretend he was still a part of her.

Becca rolled, covering Rick with her body and moving against him.

His voice held a strangled quality when he said, "This isn't right."

Holding his gaze, she said, "Nothing's been right for six days. I can't eat, I can't sleep. Before today, I couldn't cry…except for when I broke the glasses. And you took that small comfort from me. You *owe* me."

Rick's shock mirrored her own. It was such an un-Becca-like thing to say.

She didn't give him time to refuse. She captured his mouth with hers. His protest was smothered by her onslaught, the dance of her tongue inviting him, allowing him the illusion of choice. But already she was hot and wet and proclaiming what she needed. She moved her hips against him as she reached to unbutton his dress pants.

Emotions flooded her. Anger. Remorse. Need. The raw energy of being alive. And the power of being in control. Because Gabe's death had proven she had absolutely no control over the course of her life. Only this small moment in time.

Becca was determined to experience it all. She reveled in cupping her palm against the front of his pants, but the fabric was in the way. She needed to feel him, warm, pulsing, *alive*.

Closing her eyes, she unzipped his pants and encircled him with her hand.

She ignored the harsh sound of his indrawn breath and focused on the life beneath her fingertips.

"Bec, this isn't—"

"Shh." She opened her eyes, holding his gaze. "Please help me to forget this awful day."

He grasped her wrists. "Think about what you're asking."

"Don't you understand? I can't think. Because if I do, I'll have to admit that Gabe is never coming back." Becca angrily dashed away the moisture on her cheeks, leaning close and shifting so she straddled him. Her voice was low and hoarse when she said, "We don't think. We just feel. Anything but hopelessness. Help me, Rick?"

BECCA'S PLEA cut through Rick's confusion and went straight to his groin. Where her closeness had initially stimulated an automatic response, now he wanted *her* with a ferocity that nearly unhinged him. Instinct guided him as he pushed her dress up over her hips, groaning at the sight of her black thigh-high stockings against her pale skin.

The only thing Rick knew was that if he didn't sink into her right now, he was going to die.

Becca leaned close and he cradled the back of her neck with his hand, drawing her down for a deep, scorching kiss. Her fevered response almost sent him over the edge. He groped her thigh and higher, his fingers searching for the panties he knew stood between him and that wet, warm place where he needed to be.

As if sensing his loss of control, Becca drew back with a moan of frustration, snagging her panties and trying to wiggle out of them. He couldn't wait that long.

Then he realized he was still wearing his briefs. He thanked his lucky stars he was ambidextrous as he freed himself while fumbling for the wallet in his back pocket.

"Done!" Becca crowed, tossing aside her panties.

Black, he noticed.

She straddled him again, maneuvering so that his tip was nestled against her warm, moist, totally ready entrance.

His body surged, intent on answering her invitation in a big way. Everything seemed surreal, as if it were happening to someone else. Suddenly the woman who had been his friend for years was almost a stranger. The last shred of reassuring familiarity exploded into white-hot need.

"Protection." That was Rick's last rational thought as he retrieved the condom and ripped open the packet with his teeth.

Becca threw back her head and undulated her hips, torturing him with the promise of completion so close at hand. She made impatient little noises that had him wanting her all the more.

Rick rolled the condom on—at least he was pretty sure he rolled it on—the split second before Becca lowered herself onto him. Or maybe it was right before he grasped her hips and plunged into her. It was all such a blur, he could never be totally sure. He only knew that he was finally exactly where he needed to be.

CHAPTER TWO

RICK GLANCED UP from a sheaf of rental agreements in time to see Becca enter the small reception area. The support staff and rental agents crowded around her, offering hugs of encouragement.

It had been a week since Gabe's funeral and Rick was still in shock. Saying a final goodbye to his friend had been wrenching. Almost as wrenching was his own behavior afterward.

Becca glanced in his direction and their gazes connected through the glass. He nodded. She waved hesitantly and turned away. It was one of the few times he'd noticed Becca being reserved. She usually had an open, girl-next-door quality that drew people to her.

Releasing a sigh of relief, Rick hoped she would leave without coming to see him. He had no idea what he would say to her. Should he apologize? Ask if she was okay? Pretending it never happened wasn't an option. He only wished his own emotions weren't so confused. Guilt was at the top of the list, along with a slightly foolish feeling for losing it that way. He'd crossed a line.

His hopes of avoiding a confrontation were dashed a few minutes later when Becca tapped on his door and stepped inside, closing the door behind her.

A part of him was afraid she might want a repeat performance. But, having analyzed the situation from every possible angle, he found that unlikely.

"I thought we should talk about what happened after the wake," she said.

"Becca, I—"

She raised her hand to stop him. "I'm so sorry, Rick. I put you in a horrible position, took advantage of our friendship…dishonored my husband." The catch in her voice made him wince, as did her remorse.

Rick stood up, uncertain whether or not to go to her. "I'm as much to blame as you."

She gave him a warning look. "No, you're not. I threw myself at you…I don't know what came over me. But I apologize and hope we can work together without this affecting the business."

He admired the way she stood straight and accepted responsibility. He'd known Becca for more than ten years, though, so her attitude shouldn't have surprised him. Her integrity was rock solid. Being seduced by her a few hours after her husband's funeral didn't erase that knowledge.

"You were out of your mind with grief. I...should have reacted better."

Her eyes blazed. "You reacted *exactly* how I needed you to react. I nearly begged you, remember?"

"That part's a little hazy. I just remember it seemed like the right thing to do at the time."

Maybe that was a simplified version, but it was better than nothing. In those moments on the kitchen floor with her, all he'd known was that he needed what she'd offered and she'd obviously needed him. Not for physical release. But to connect with another living, breathing being when so much had been taken from them.

Becca stepped closer to his desk, leaning forward, her blond hair falling to her shoulders. Her voice was soft when she said, "We can't go back and undo it, no matter how badly we may want to."

"Yeah."

"And I know we can never totally act as if it never happened."

Rick knew he would never, *ever* forget Becca

holding him as if he was the center of her universe. "No, probably not."

"But I need to ask a favor."

"Anything." It was an automatic gut response.

"Have you told anyone?"

"Of course not."

"I didn't think so, but I had to check."

"And this favor?"

"It would hurt innocent people if this got out. My children, my in-laws. They might think it was some reflection on my feelings for Gabe. I loved my husband with my whole heart. Please don't tell anyone what happened." Her voice was husky, reminding him of the way she'd murmured in his ear as she'd made love with him. Even then, he'd understood that Becca was Gabe's forever. What Rick had experienced with her had been an aberration.

An intense aberration he couldn't quite get off his mind. But that was his problem, not hers.

"I won't tell anyone, Becca."

"Promise?"

"Promise."

BECCA SIGHED with relief when she settled herself in the driver's seat of the minivan, hoping she could avoid Akron rush hour. Her conversation with Rick had been tense, but she'd deserved every second of discomfort. He'd been gracious, all things considered.

Stopping at the neighborhood grocery store on her way home, she intended to run in, get a few things and leave. But she saw several people she knew, and the condolences, though thoughtful, seemed to go on forever. Still, she considered herself lucky to have so many people who cared about her.

It was nearly two o'clock when Becca walked through the door at home. The kids would be there in two hours and the house would erupt in controlled chaos.

"I was starting to worry," Irene said. "I thought you were only going to the salon for a half day."

Becca kissed her mother-in-law on the cheek and placed the bags on the counter. "I'm fine. I had a few things I needed to clear up at the rental agency after work. And I stopped at the grocery store."

"Surely we've got enough meals in the freezer to last a month. Or years."

"Yes." Becca smiled. The way the condolence casseroles seemed to multiply in the freezer was an ongoing joke. "But we still use toilet tissue, soap and other things."

"Let me get my purse."

She hugged the older woman. "Hang on to your cash. It's all stuff I would have had to buy anyway."

Irene frowned. "We need to pay our way. It's not easy expanding your family by two and we don't ever want to be a burden. We promised five years ago to contribute."

"You're never a burden. You contribute by paying the electric and water bills. And by being here for the kids after school. That helps more than you will ever know."

"I wish you'd let us do more. Especially now...with Gabe...gone." Her eyes clouded. "Jim and I should probably be looking into other arrangements. Maybe a retirement village."

"Nonsense. You're still an important part of this family. It wouldn't be the same around here without you."

Irene cupped Becca's cheek with her hand. "You're a good girl. I'm so happy Gabe found you. You made a perfect couple."

"Yes, we did." Her voice wavered. She tried to avoid the sense of hopelessness that seemed to always be hovering close by these days. "I only wish I'd had one last chance to tell him how much I loved him."

"He knew. You were the world to him."

Becca was at risk of losing her composure if

they discussed Gabe a moment longer. Trying to change the subject, she said, "Hey, you and Jim provided him with an example of the perfect marriage."

"That takes work as you well know. Speaking of work, I better call Jim in from the workshop so he can help bring in the groceries."

"Let him continue with his project. I only had these two bags."

"It's good for him to feel needed."

Becca patted Irene's arm. "I know. That's why I'm grateful for his help. But today it's not necessary."

"Don't feel you have to do everything yourself. Accept help when people offer."

Becca turned away and pretended to check the contents of the grocery sack. "I do."

"Only when you feel you have no other choice."

Glancing up, she found Irene watching her. "It's…hard. Gabe and I were a team, a unit. Now, I'm not sure what I am."

"You're a woman who has had a terrible loss. A woman who works hard to keep it together on her own. Sometimes, accepting help is the greatest gift you can give someone you love."

Becca would have agreed with her, as long as it was someone else on the receiving end.

Helping Gabe's parents was as much a part of her as taking care of her children. And she would do the same thing for her father and his wife when they weren't able to live alone anymore.

But asking for help was one thing Becca couldn't seem to do. Except for asking—no, demanding—that Rick make it all go away for a few moments the night of Gabe's funeral.

Becca's gaze was drawn to the tiled floor where she'd made love to Rick. Her stomach protested.

"Are you okay, dear?" Irene asked.

"Yes. I was just thinking…" And hoping guilt wasn't written all over her face, like a scarlet *A*. She knew Irene would be horrified if she ever found out. The thought of losing her respect made Becca's heart ache.

But no one would ever know. Rick had promised.

Becca would be left to wrestle with her conscience alone. In this very kitchen, she'd managed to betray not only Gabe, but Rick. How would she ever forgive herself for such a huge abuse of trust?

When she contemplated what Rick probably thought of her, Becca inwardly cringed.

It didn't matter.

Who was she kidding? It mattered a great deal. She didn't want to lose his friendship over a moment of insanity. It was almost a compulsion these days to keep the people who'd known and loved Gabe as close as possible. As if, in some way, it kept Gabe close, too.

A WEEK LATER, Rick waited in the booth at Coco's Restaurant. His reason for inviting Becca had been purely practical. They needed to discuss business in a neutral setting. The office was out, because he didn't want to spook the employees if anyone heard about belt-tightening. And Becca's house was definitely not a good idea.

He stood as she approached the table, admiring the vibrant swing of her blond hair, her confident stride and ready smile. The lines of strain were barely noticeable. But the fact that she'd lost weight was readily evident and he worried.

That was the other reason for inviting her to lunch. At least he was sure she'd eat one good meal today instead of forgetting to take care of herself while she looked after everyone else.

Rick grasped her hands and kissed her quickly on the cheek. "Hi. No problem with traffic?"

"Not a bit. This was a great idea." Her eyes held a trace of wariness, though.

He wondered if she would think it was such

a good idea when he was finished imparting his news.

"How are the kids doing?" he asked as they sat down.

"It depends on the hour. They seem to take turns having meltdowns in their own way. It's exhausting trying to gauge who's having a hard time and what I should do to make it right."

"Not a whole lot you can do. Except listen and let them know you're there."

"But I'm their mother. I should be able to offer words of wisdom that make their pain bearable. I've spouted the 'we're in this together' stuff until they're tired of hearing it. And to be honest, grief is a pretty solitary pursuit. No matter how badly I want to be there for them, a lot of it they're going to have to work out in their own time in their own way."

Rick nodded. "Same goes for you."

"The children have to be my focus right now. I don't have the luxury of falling to pieces."

"I remember when Kayla was a teen. It made me feel so helpless when I realized that she would ultimately have to find her own way. My ex-wife and I just stood there with our hearts on our sleeves, hoping like crazy she'd ask us for guidance. And when she didn't, providing it anyway."

"You and Valerie did a good job. Kayla seemed like a nice girl the few times she's come to the office to visit."

"Yes, I don't see her nearly often enough. But she's got her own life. I guess I should be grateful she got a job in Akron after she graduated from NYU."

Becca reached across the table and touched his arm. "I'm sorry. I seem to have lost every ounce of tact I once had. She's just doing the usual separation thing, trying to be an adult."

Awareness rippled through him, reminding him she had once touched him in a more intimate way.

As if sensing his thoughts, Becca quickly withdrew her hand.

The waitress arrived and took their order and the awkward moment passed.

"Tell me the real reason for the lunch invitation."

Rick cleared his throat. "There are some changes around the office I need to discuss with you."

"Changes?"

"Personnel. I brought the books for you to take home and look at this evening. Gabe's only been gone two weeks and I'm swamped. We're going to lose customers if our service suffers—you know how competitive the rental business is."

"I know you've had a lot on your plate. Can we hire someone to…fill Gabe's position?"

"We can't afford two salaries for one position."

Becca paled. "You've continued to pay his salary to us. I have to admit, I didn't stop to think what that would mean."

"Believe me, I'd like to keep on paying his salary indefinitely. If business were booming, we could. But you know we're putting most of our profit back into the agency."

"You have to do what's best for the company. Hire someone to take Gabe's place. We'll… manage somehow."

He could tell from the panic in her eyes that she had no idea how her family would manage.

"What about Gabe's life insurance? Will that tide you over until we can pay you a dividend?"

"He let the policy lapse."

Rick swore under his breath. How could Gabe have been so careless?

Simple. Gabe hadn't intended to drop dead at forty-two.

There was no way Rick could pull the rug from beneath Becca. He'd simply have to continue with eighty-hour workweeks and hope for the best. "Forget I said anything. Maybe I can delegate some of Gabe's duties."

"What about me? Why don't I pick up some of the slack?"

"Becca, you've got a full-time job of your own at the salon, plus the agency's accounts receivable and three kids who are grieving for their father. With elderly in-laws, your plate is already too full."

He didn't add that it would be nearly impossible to work that closely with her and not be reminded of what they'd shared. And what he feared they'd lost.

Their meals arrived, giving them a moment of respite from the heavy topic.

"This business meant the world to Gabe," she said. "He wouldn't want it jeopardized."

"He wouldn't want his family jeopardized, either."

"Then why did he let the policy lapse?" Becca's confusion and frustration were evident in her voice.

"You meant the world to him, Becca."

"Why does everyone keep saying that? If I meant the world to him he wouldn't have left me."

"He didn—"

"Logically, I know he didn't choose to leave

us. I know he never intended to need that policy, either. But he did. And I can't help but feel a little…shell-shocked." Blinking away tears, she said, "Things were so good between us. I can't believe he's gone, Rick."

He patted her hand. His voice was rough when he said, "I know. Neither can I."

"You know what scares me most? That I might give up. That I'll curl up in a ball and give up. What will my children do then?"

Rick rubbed her knuckles with his thumb. His eyes were warm with concern. "Becca, I can't begin to imagine how hard it is for you. But I've known you during good times and bad, and the one thing I can tell you is that you're strong. You'll get through this."

"I'm a fake, Rick. Inside, I'm just a scared little girl who wants Gabe to come home and make it all right." She glanced away. "But even if by some miracle he did, I'd never be able to look him in the eye. Because of what I did."

"What *we* did."

Becca wiped her eyes. "I blame myself. The guilt wakes me up in the middle of the night."

"Becca, listen to me. The guilt will eat you alive if you don't acknowledge that, technically, we did nothing wrong."

"Oh, please. Technically, my husband was barely in the grave and I seduced his best friend."

"Shh." Rick glanced around. "Calm down."

Her eyes narrowed. "I'm very calm. You seem to be in the unenviable position of being the one person with whom I can be honest. The one person who has seen me at my worst during this crisis and still manages not to hate me as much as I hate myself." She stood. "I'm going to leave before I unload more on you than either of us is comfortable with. Give me the books and I'll return them tomorrow."

Rick complied, watching helplessly as she stalked out of the restaurant. Her half-eaten meal seemed to mock him.

And her parting shots replayed in his mind. Why on earth had she chosen to trust him? He had the feeling she didn't know the answer any better than he did.

Rick also wondered what she could have possibly unloaded that would have shocked him more than being seduced by her in such a direct, no-holds-barred manner.

He tossed some bills on the table and went after her. Not to confront her, but to make sure she was okay.

CHAPTER THREE

BECCA WALKED OUTSIDE into the sunshine and felt the world spin. She steadied herself against the restaurant wall, hoping Rick hadn't noticed, as he came striding up beside her.

Quickly righting herself, she glanced sideways at him.

He seemed lost in thought and didn't comment.

When they reached her car, he kissed her on the cheek and closed the door behind her. Then stood and waited for her to start the car.

She should have found his concern reassuring. But it simply made her feel trapped. Because no matter how hard she tried, circumstances seemed to be spinning out of control. The lightheadedness wasn't normal and she was afraid to face what it might mean.

Becca backed the car out of the space and waved. She almost made it home before her stomach rebelled and she had to pull off on a side street. Finally, her stomach settled and she was able to finish the drive.

Becca ignored the panic waiting to engulf her. She reassured herself with the thought that the queasiness had started when she'd been notified of Gabe's death. It was a reaction to stress, nothing more.

Becca managed to keep the tears at bay until she reached home. Pulling into the garage, she pushed the control and lowered the door behind her, then unbuckled her seat belt by rote.

But her hand hovered over the ignition. It would be so easy to leave the car running and drift off into unconsciousness. There wouldn't be any more difficult conversations, impossible decisions or agonizing days and achingly empty nights. She wouldn't have to sleep in Gabe's T-shirts simply to remind herself what it was like to have him near. And she wouldn't have to dread the next forty or so years, pining for the man who had captured her heart so long ago.

When Becca thought of all the birthdays, holidays and special occasions stretching before her, the ache grew unbearable. She couldn't imagine attending their children's graduations without Gabe. Couldn't stand the thought of Maya not having her father walk her down the aisle at her wedding. Couldn't believe Gabe wouldn't be there to grow old with her.

Closing her eyes, Becca felt the seemingly never-ending tears wet her face. She tried to recall how Gabe had looked on their anniversary cruise when they'd found their love renewed, stronger than ever.

Her heart ached so badly it seemed to radiate through her entire torso. Becca wrapped her arms around her waist and rocked.

Simply staying in the car and waiting for the fumes to collect would be a solution to her suffering. A very final solution. But, suddenly, she could see her children, heartbroken and lost, at yet another funeral. Suicide would leave scars that might not ever heal.

Becca opened her eyes and twisted the key with more force than was necessary. She was no quitter and she had no intention of leaving her children to mourn two parents instead of one.

In that moment, Becca felt a calmness wash over her. It was as if her soul had returned to her body after hovering above. She felt totally present for the first time in two weeks. As if she had found renewed purpose beyond the constant pain. Whatever the reason, Becca sensed she'd turned an important corner. No longer a helpless victim of fate, she would do everything within her power to make life right again for her children.

RICK'S STEPS SLOWED as he approached his office the next morning. Squaring his shoulders, he prepared for another difficult conversation.

"Becca, what are you doing here this morning?"

"I'm here to work. I've decided to take over Gabe's job. He loved this place and wanted to build a legacy for our children. And I intend to make that happen."

Rick went around his desk, sitting. He took a long drink from his travel mug, wishing it was something stronger than coffee. "I told you I'd make it work. There's no need for you to do this."

"Yes, there is. You can't hire anyone else without giving them Gabe's salary. We can't live without Gabe's salary. I'll cut back my hours at the hair salon, keep only my best customers and take over for Gabe. With social security, we should be able to make it."

"You've been around the business a lot, but there would still be so much to learn."

"I'm a quick learner. And we could hire someone part-time for accounts receivable as profits allow."

"There will be long hours. You need to be there for your kids."

"In a perfect world, I could drop everything to ease this transition for my children. Unfortunately, it's not a perfect world and I need to find the best solution. Gabe's parents offered to pick up more of the slack at home. We can do it. And David works here part-time, so I might see him more often."

Rick noticed a new resolve in her voice. While he admired her confidence, he didn't want the business to suffer if she wasn't able to tackle it all. "Let me have some time to think it over."

"What's to think over? You may own controlling interest, but only by two percent. This business is as much mine as it is yours."

He'd never missed Gabe more than at this moment. Their partnership had grown and evolved into an organic, symbiotic relationship. With Becca, he'd be starting from square one. And with a woman he'd slept with, no less. It was a recipe for disaster.

But she had a point about ownership. Technically, he could make unilateral decisions, but it didn't bode well for keeping the business together. The last thing he wanted to do was be forced to sell.

Running his hand through his hair, he asked, "There's nothing I can say to dissuade you?"

"Nothing." Her voice was emphatic.

"I can check with the bank about a business loan or see if I can take out a second mortgage on my house. Maybe then I could buy out your share."

"No, Rick, absolutely not. I'm here, I'm staying and I intend to be an active partner. It's the least I can do for my children. The least I can do to honor Gabe."

How could he say no when she put it that way?

He couldn't. But he could at least buy himself time. Very few people could maintain the kind of commitments Becca described. Maybe she would eventually be forced to admit it wasn't a good idea.

"Why don't we give it a trial run? Maybe sixty days and then reevaluate?"

"Deal." Becca extended her hand.

He shook, wondering what the hell he'd gotten himself into. "Deal."

CHAPTER FOUR

RICK CONNECTED to the ball with a vicious swing. It ricocheted off the wall and came back low.

He sprinted a few feet to lob it this time. Wiping the sweat from his eyes, he returned with another lob. The lob wasn't a strategic play, it was borne from the sheer necessity of playing racquetball by himself.

He'd canceled his court time twice after Gabe's death. But now, he needed the release of physical exertion. And not the kind that immediately came to mind. Because when he thought of that kind of exertion, he thought of Becca.

His next shot was low and lethal. Dodging left, he barely missed being hit. Half an hour later, he couldn't catch his breath.

Was he having a heart attack?

Before, he would have brushed off the thought. He was too young, too fit for that to happen. But Gabe had been young and apparently fit and now he was dead.

Exiting the court, he draped a towel around his neck, trying not to look for Gabe. He half expected to turn his head and see his friend standing there, grinning.

"Hey, Jensen."

Rick turned, but no Gabe. Instead it was a guy he'd seen around the gym.

"Hey."

"I heard about Gabe. Sorry, man."

"Thanks."

Rick couldn't recall the guy's name. Rob, Bob, something like that.

"I'm Bill Connors. My partner and I have the next court time."

"Oh, yeah. See ya around." Rick turned, unwilling to watch the twosome enjoy a kick-ass game when his partner was six feet under.

"Thing is, I was wondering what you'll be doing with your court time. Didn't see you here last week. Me and my buddies wouldn't mind taking it off your hands."

Rick slowly turned to face Bill, his hand clenching his racquet handle. It was all he could do to keep from taking the guy's head off. He had lost his best friend, his business and racquetball partner. He'd be damned if he was going to lose his court time, too.

"I've got a new partner starting next week,"

Rick lied. "But I'll keep you in mind if I decide to give it up."

"I'd appreciate it."

"No problem."

Rick exited the parking lot faster than was necessary, anger buzzing through his system. The problem was, he didn't know why he was so pissed off. Maybe because he had absolutely nobody with whom he wanted to partner up on the racquetball court. Rick was the kind of guy who was content with one close friend. That had been Gabe. No wonder he felt the loss so keenly.

When he reached the rental agency ten minutes later, Rick swung his car into the parking lot and sighed. There was a pickup parked in his space beneath the shade tree.

Finding a spot at the back of the lot, Rick was in a pretty foul mood. First with Bill trying to take his court time, now with David Smith stealing his parking space. It seemed as if the kid had been challenging him a lot lately.

His irritation grew darker as he entered the agency and saw the light on in his office.

He nodded and said a curt good-morning to the Saturday staff.

His suspicions were confirmed when he walked into his office.

"David." It came out more a challenge than a greeting.

"Hey, Rick."

"You want to get out of my seat?"

David's chin came up. "It's my father's company, too."

"Yes, and your father has a desk. I suggest you use it."

"It's…weird not to see him there."

The challenge was gone and all Rick saw was the young boy who had done cannonballs into the pool the first time Rick had been invited to the Smith house for a party.

Even then, he'd envied the way the Smiths had fun together. And how people seemed to flock to their home, where impromptu parties were common.

Rick cleared his throat. "Yeah, it's kind of weird for me, too. I expect to see your dad walk through the door all the time."

"Like he's at lunch or something."

Rick nodded. He stood behind David, willing him out of his chair and feeling guilty about it. "I bet you can scare up an empty desk somewhere in the office."

"All right already. I'm moving."

"Good. Oh, and David? Don't park in my space again."

"You're on a real power trip, huh?"

"You know the rules."

"Yeah, well, I'm tired of it always being your way. It's our business as much as it's yours. It's time I stepped up to the plate as the man of the family. I'm gonna talk to my mom about me taking over my dad's job instead of her."

"I can think of several reasons that wouldn't be a good idea, the first of which is your age. Twenty may seem mature to you, but believe me there's a lot to learn. And I can't imagine your mother would be happy about you quitting college."

"Probably not. But this is something I need to do. I can't just stand by and do nothing while my family sinks. If I take over Dad's position, then my mom can work at the salon full-time and nothing's changed. We can make it."

Rick had to wonder about David seeming so well informed about the family finances.

"Your mother and I can discuss increasing your hours if she thinks you can handle it and still carry a full course load."

"That's not what I'm talking about and you know it. I'll quit school. She'll know that it's the best way. You'll see."

Rick felt a headache forming behind his eyes. He hoped like crazy that David was wrong. But

Becca had been acting out of character since Gabe died. Did David know something Rick didn't?

IT WAS NEARLY three o'clock by the time Becca made it into the agency. She'd done upsweeps for a wedding party, run home, made lunch for the kids, taken sixteen-year-old Maya to dance class, mopped up a mess after ten-year-old Aaron had washed the dog in the upstairs tub, then picked up Maya from dance class.

Then she'd listened to Maya's sobs about a lost dance solo for the upcoming recital. Becca had to wonder if her daughter's hysteria was caused more by fallout from Gabe's death than losing the solo. With teenage girls, it was hard to tell. Emotions swung from one extreme to the other, with barely any advance notice. It was like trying to grab hold of a funnel cloud.

Sighing with relief, Becca was pleased to have the relative peace of the rental agency to look forward to.

She waved to the agents and went into Gabe's office, where she found David.

"Hi, sweetheart. Isn't it about time for you to head home?"

"Yeah, but I'm trying to put in more hours. Rick said it was okay."

Becca suppressed a flash of annoyance. "It would have been nice if he'd talked to me first."

"I was the one who brought it up. Anyway, I think he was just trying to keep me quiet. I told him I wanted to take over Dad's job so you wouldn't have to."

"You told him what? I thought I made myself clear. School first. Once you have your degree, then we'll see what we can do."

"We can't afford college. My tuition is expensive. I could be contributing to the family finances instead of draining them."

Becca scraped her bangs off her face. "I'll work it out somehow. And I'm going to take on your dad's job. Don't worry about your tuition *or* the family finances."

"Mom, I've heard you on the phone to Uncle Royce. I know Dad didn't have any life insurance. How can I go to school when I know we need the money?"

"We'll do fine. I'm drawing your father's salary now."

"And losing half of your own."

"Once I get things down here, I might be able to spend more time in the salon."

"Why? I can help."

"No, and that's final. Your father wanted you to have a college education. I want you to have a college education."

David grumbled, but tidied up his mess. "I won't be home for dinner."

Neither will I.

Truth be told, she had enough work to keep her busy till late into the night. But shared dinners were the glue that kept a family together.

"Where will you be?" Becca asked.

"I'm taking Brittany out to dinner. It's her birthday."

Becca nodded. "Have fun. And be careful."

"I always am."

"I know you are." Just as she knew he was a normal twenty-year-old kid who occasionally didn't think things through. She'd always feared a phone call in the middle of the night saying something had happened to one of her children.

Since Gabe's death, it had become almost a compulsion. She worried until she heard David and Maya come up the stairs and enter their own rooms. Only then would the dread ease.

David kissed her on the cheek before leaving.

She went to Rick's office, knocking on the door frame as she entered.

He glanced up, his expression inscrutable. "Hi, Becca. I didn't expect to see you today."

"Gabe usually worked Saturday afternoons."

"Yeah, but you have the kids and all their activities."

Becca shrugged, hoping she didn't look half as exhausted as she felt. "I'll do both."

"Are you sure you're okay?"

"I'm fine."

"You look like you haven't slept for days."

"Gee, thanks, you really know how to make a woman feel beautiful."

"You're always beautiful, Becca." Rick flushed, as if realizing what he'd said. "But you're going to burn out if you're not careful. Gabe would never forgive me if I allowed that to happen."

"Gabe would understand why I have to do this."

"I'm not so sure. He'd hate to see how hard you're pushing yourself."

"There's no other way. Now, do you have a few minutes to sit down and go over what I can expect in the next couple weeks as we prepare to return leased vehicles?"

"Pull a chair over. I'll show you what I have so far. Then you can go with me to the body shop and we can check on repair status."

"Good."

For the next hour Rick explained how the

system worked. "The factory won't take back vehicles with extensive repairs or obvious damage," he told her once he'd run through the procedures.

"So we're stuck with them?"

"We'll have to sell them at auction, probably at a loss." He handed her a computer printout. "These cars should be on the lot today. We'll thoroughly inspect them and avoid renting them out again if possible."

"What if we do have to rent them?"

"We'll want to reinspect them even more closely than usual. Come on, I'll show you what to look for."

They went out on the lot.

"I also pulled the repair history on each vehicle, so we can eyeball the repairs. Everything has to be pristine. The new cars will be arriving as these leave, so it's going to be chaotic." He grinned.

"Why do I get the feeling you thrive on this?"

"Probably because I do."

"This process used to kind of stress Gabe out. Not that he complained or anything. He wouldn't have wanted me to worry. I wonder if he'd still be here if I'd worried more."

"You can't second-guess yourself, Becca."

"How can I *not* second-guess myself?"

"Focus on what you can do. You've got some pretty intense challenges right now."

They checked the vehicles one by one, a time-consuming job with a midsize fleet. Fortunately, many were rented out at the moment. Becca was amazed at how easily Rick could find a flawed repair or minor damage.

He shook his head. "Roger's usually not this careless. He's been at it for so long, he could do bodywork in his sleep."

"Gabe thought the world of him. Said he was the best in the business and we were very fortunate to have him run our body shop."

"He's got a couple kids working with him to help get the cars ready for return. This must've got past him. I'll talk to him about watching the guys more closely."

"See this fender." Rick squatted, pointing. "Run your palm over it."

Becca knelt next to him on the asphalt, glad she'd worn jeans today. She ran her hand over the fender the way she'd seen him do it. "I can feel it's rougher there. And it looks like the paint is bubbled up."

"Yep, that'll need to be sanded and repainted. If we had to send out the repairs, this would be a substantial expense. But since we have our own shop, that keeps costs down."

Nodding, Becca said, "Yes, one of the women at the salon was rear-ended, a fender bender really, and repairs cost over a thousand dollars."

"Absolutely." Glancing at his watch, he said, "I gotta run. I'm meeting Valerie for drinks."

"You two have the most amicable divorce I've ever seen."

Rick stood, brushing off his hands. Grinning, he said, "Too bad the marriage wasn't this amicable. We just get together once a month to compare notes on Kayla."

Becca rose, too, bracing her hand against the car, hoping she didn't sway.

"Are you okay?" Rick steadied her.

She managed to smile. "Fine. Just stood up too quickly."

"This dizziness worries me. And you've lost weight. Maybe you should see someone about it."

"I'm really fine." She smiled brightly. "Besides, I've got a checkup next week. I'll mention it to my doctor then."

"Be sure you do. After what happened to Gabe, I'm kind of jumpy about my friends not feeling well."

"I'll talk to the doctor, I promise. And thanks

for caring enough to nag. I'm fortunate to have friends like you."

Though just this once, she wished Rick were a little less observant.

CHAPTER FIVE

A WEEK LATER, Dr. Barker finished the examination. "Go ahead and get dressed, then meet me in my office."

"That sounds…ominous."

The doctor smiled, kindness in her warm brown eyes. "Not at all. Just a better place to talk."

"I read the material in your waiting room about perimenopause and that certainly describes some of the symptoms I'm having. Fatigue, mood swings, difficulty concentrating, decreased appetite…or it could have something to do with stress."

"We'll discuss it in my office." The doctor closed the door behind her.

Becca dressed as quickly as possible, her fingers fumbling with the buttons on her blouse. She avoided looking at the diagrams of a woman's reproductive organs on the wall.

One of the drawbacks to having her ob-gyn handling her general checkup.

When she emerged from the examination room, the nurse took her to Dr. Barker's office.

The doctor glanced up from a file and smiled warmly. "Have a seat."

Becca sat in the padded chair, wishing they could dispense with formalities and get right to the point.

"We checked your hormone levels to see if perimenopause might be the culprit. We also checked for pregnancy hormones."

"Pregnancy? No, that couldn't…"

But it could have happened and that's why she'd been trying to avoid panicking. Trying not to think about it at all.

"Becca, you're not perimenopausal. You're pregnant."

The room spun and Becca felt as if she might be sick.

"I understand the timing may not be the most opportune…"

"No, it's not." She started to tick off items on her fingers. "I'm forty-one, recently widowed, working two jobs to keep food on the table and supporting three children and my two elderly in-laws."

Dr. Barker reached across the desk and grasped her hand. "I'm sorry. There are options…"

Becca drew back in horror. "Abortion? Absolutely not."

"Adoption."

"No, I couldn't live with myself. I'll work through this. Raise the child myself. H-how far along am I?"

"We'll need to do an ultrasound to determine that. You said you haven't missed any periods?"

"No, but my last one was very light. I thought it was because of stress."

"Maybe this baby will bring you joy—a gift from your late husband."

"Yes, of course."

Becca was barely aware of grabbing her purse and fleeing the office.

She couldn't face going back to the agency. She called Rick and, wonder of wonders, something worked out right for her. Her call went straight to his voice mail.

"Hi, Rick, it's Becca. I have some stuff I'd like to take care of from home, so I won't be back today as planned. I'll be in bright and early tomorrow morning."

There, her voice hadn't even wavered.

No need to call home because her family

wouldn't expect her until dinnertime. What she did need was some time alone to think.

She drove through Cuyahoga Falls and headed out of town, seeking serenity at Cuyahoga Valley National Park.

Her thoughts bounced around like a frantic rabbit as she drove. But she wouldn't allow them to get out of hand. Even now, safety was paramount. Maybe even more than before.

A short time later, she pulled into the parking lot near her favorite covered bridge, a spot that seemed to take her back to the simpler times when the historic bridge was built. A time before progress in Ohio meant paved roads and shopping malls.

She got out and walked, simply walked, allowing the thoughts to come cascading in.

How in the world had this happened? She and Gabe had used condoms as protection for years, but had gotten progressively lax. Becca had secretly welcomed the idea of another child and Gabe had been on the fence. Until two nights before he died, when he'd laughingly said they'd take their chances.

Why then? Had Gabe had some premonition of his death?

Becca smiled, touching her stomach. It

would be wonderful to have one more part of Gabe live on.

But what if the baby wasn't Gabe's? A wave of nausea made her tremble. No, it wasn't possible. She remembered how insistent Rick had been about using protection, even in the throes of the most spontaneous lovemaking she'd ever experienced. Becca would be forever grateful for his consideration, because she'd been in no state of mind to consider the ramifications.

In his way, he'd given her a gift, too. Because she could, with certainty, know this baby was Gabe's.

RICK FINISHED WORK around seven. He probably should swing by the gym, but he couldn't seem to shake the feeling that there was something going on with Becca.

Nodding to his staff, he grabbed a few files on his way out.

As he walked up the Smith driveway a short time later, Rick told himself he was worried about a friend, pure and simple. It was normal to feel responsible for his best friend's widow.

Wasn't it?

He rang the doorbell and waited.

Aaron answered the door and hollered, "Mom, it's Rick."

The boy left the door open, so Rick stepped into the entryway.

Becca staggered in, yawning.

"Hi, Rick. I must've fallen asleep on the couch."

Even half-asleep and with dark circles under her eyes, Becca was beautiful.

Shifting, he said, "I brought you the damage files. Thought you might want to look them over."

"Thank you."

"Everything go okay at the doctor's today?"

"Fine. I'm healthy as a horse."

But she didn't look healthy. She looked drawn and lifeless. There was something she wasn't telling him. He'd known Becca long enough to sense when she was dancing around an issue.

He opened his mouth to protest, but Maya beat him to the punch.

Coming down the stairs, she asked, "You went to the doctor? Why didn't you tell us? Is something wrong?" There was an edge of panic in her voice.

Becca raised her chin. "Absolutely not. It was a routine checkup, nothing more."

"You'd tell us if something was wrong, wouldn't you?"

"Of course."

Becca's overbright smile told him that she would do whatever was necessary to protect her daughter. But Maya seemed mollified.

The girl gave her mother a big hug. "Okay. I love you."

"I love you, too."

Mother and daughter were about the same height, but that was where the resemblance ended. Maya was all Gabe, with an olive complexion and expressive brown eyes.

"I'm going to Trina's house to study." Maya grabbed her backpack.

"Be home by ten."

"See ya." And she walked out the door.

"They are so self-contained at that age," he commented.

"She worries too much. If I'm five minutes late, she calls. If she can't reach me on my cell, she starts to panic. I think she's afraid of losing me, too."

"I can understand that."

"Yes, but it makes things difficult sometimes." Rick hesitated.

"Do you want to come in?" Becca asked.

He had a feeling he was expected to decline, but instead said, "Sure, for a few minutes."

"Maybe there are still some cookies left in the kitchen. Come on, let's go check."

He followed her to the kitchen, admiring the ease with which she handled his sudden appearance. Their lovemaking hadn't shaken her as much as him.

Aaron was sitting at the kitchen table, his math book open in front of him.

"I thought you already finished your homework," Becca commented.

"I forgot a page."

"Hmm. Try harder to remember next time. I don't like you leaving your homework till the last minute. That makes for sloppy work." She ruffled his hair as she went to the counter. "Have a seat, Rick."

He sat at the opposite end of the table, so their talk wouldn't disturb Aaron's concentration.

"Coffee? Water?" Becca asked, placing a plate of cookies on the table.

The boy snagged the first one.

"Water's fine," Rick said.

Becca returned with two glasses of ice water and napkins.

Selecting a cookie, Rick nodded toward the plate. "Still working on the leftovers from the wake?"

Becca's smile faded as she sat down in a chair across the table from him. "They freeze well."

Gabe's mother, Irene, came in the kitchen. She glanced at him, unspoken questions in her eyes. "Hello, Rick. Good to see you again." *So soon?*

"Good to see you, too. I brought some files for Becca."

"Why don't you join us for a snack, Irene," Becca invited.

"No. But I'll steal a couple cookies and take them out to Jim."

"Is he working on something in the shop?" Rick asked.

"Yes. I haven't seen it yet—he's been very secretive about this project. But he did let it slip that it's some sort of commemorative to Gabe."

"Ah, so you're trying to catch him unawares and the cookies are your excuse?" Becca teased.

Irene stiffened. "Absolutely not. That would be an abuse of his trust. Trust is very important, don't you agree, Rick?"

Did he detect an undercurrent? Surely there was no way she could know what had happened with Becca the night of Gabe's funeral.

He forced himself not to break eye contact. "Trust is very important."

She nodded, her hand hovering over the cookies. Her stare was lethal.

He grasped at another reason for his visit. "Um, Becca, I also came by to talk to you about David."

Becca frowned. "Did he take your parking space again? I talked to him about that. If it involves him working more hours, I would prefer that he spend the time studying."

"I agree with you about the hours and I'll back you up. He seems determined to be the man of the house now that Gabe's gone."

"I don't want that for him and I'm sure Gabe wouldn't, either. I want him to have every opportunity to be a young man before he has too many responsibilities thrust on him."

"It seems to be something he's taking on himself," Rick said. "The kid's wound pretty tightly. I need to find a replacement partner for racquetball, or I'm going to lose my court time at the gym. I was thinking it might be a good outlet for David to blow off steam."

Becca smiled. "I think it's a wonderful idea."

"Hmmph." Irene made a great show of wrapping cookies in a napkin.

"What do you think, Irene?" Becca asked.

"It's fine, I guess. Nobody could replace David's father, though."

There was a moment's silence, then Rick said, "I know that."

Slowly, Irene nodded. "Good." Then she left through the back door.

"I hope Irene's feeling all right." Becca

sounded concerned. "She's not usually short with people. I've been worried about her since the funeral."

"I'm sure she's fine." As a matter of fact, he was pretty sure Irene had picked up on the vibes he'd been trying to hide, even from himself.

Because when he looked across the table at Becca, he remembered how good they'd been together.

CHAPTER SIX

BECCA TRIED TO focus on what Rick was saying. But her mind kept drifting to the news she'd received from the doctor and what it would mean to her life.

"Hey, earth to Becca."

"I'm sorry. I guess I'm still groggy from my nap."

"I better go." Rick rose and placed his glass in the sink.

For a wild instant, Becca wished she could confide in him. She needed a shoulder to lean on so badly. But Rick was the last person to rely on for emotional support. Look where it had gotten them last time.

"I'll walk you to the door." There must have been a note of desperation in her voice, because Rick raised an eyebrow.

"Thanks, I think."

"I'm not trying to get rid of you…"

"Hey, I didn't intend to stay." He ruffled

Aaron's hair on his way past. "Keep hittin' the books."

"I'm almost done."

Becca breathed a sigh of relief when she closed the door behind Rick. She found pretending everything was normal tremendously draining.

After helping Aaron with the rest of his homework, she tucked him into bed and ran a couple loads of laundry, then sat down on the couch in the great room.

Glancing at her watch, she sighed. It was nearly time for Maya to be home from studying. Becca closed her eyes for just a moment…

She awakened to the sound of glass breaking. Fear brought her instantly awake. Was it an intruder?

But her eyes focused on Maya clumsily trying to scoop up pieces of Becca's favorite vase.

"I'm sorry, Mom. I was trying to be quiet, but I bumped into the table, and the vase…" Maya swayed. "Broke."

Becca went to her daughter and was dismayed when she smelled beer.

Grasping Maya's arm, she asked, "Have you been drinking?"

"No!" But the teenager hiccuped and giggled. "I guess I'm busted."

"Where'd you get the beer?"

"Nowhere."

"Maya, I want to know the truth. Where were you tonight and how did you get the beer?"

"I told you, I was at Trina's house. Her dad keeps a whole fridgeful."

What had happened to her levelheaded honor student?

"Maya, this isn't like you."

"No big deal. Everybody does it."

"Not you. We'll discuss your punishment in the morning when you're more likely to remember, but you can bet you'll be grounded for starters."

"Sure, Mom, whatever." Maya wove her way to the stairs and managed to navigate them on legs that were probably steadier than her mother's. "G'night."

"'Night, baby," she murmured, wishing her daughter was in fact a baby again. So Becca could keep her safe from harm.

RICK THOUGHT he might just expire on the spot. His lungs burned, his muscles screamed in protest, and sweat nearly blinded him.

But he would not give up.

He lunged for the shot and managed to return it cleanly.

David loped a few steps and sent it zinging back with awesome power.

Rick raised his racket in self-defense, sending a low ball to the corner. It took a wicked hop.

David cursed as he lunged, missing the ball by a hairbreadth.

"I win." Rick hoped the kid couldn't hear him wheeze. Man, he was getting too old to compete with the young guys.

"Lucky shot, old man." David slapped him on the back.

Rick finally gave in and bent at the waist, trying to catch his breath. A few moments later, he straightened. "Not too old…to give you…a run for your money."

"Hey, maybe you better sit down." The concern in David's voice told Rick he was truly over the hill at forty-three.

"I'm…fine."

"You're not, um, going to have a heart attack, are you?"

"No way." But really, how could he make a promise like that? "At least, I hope not."

"I should have gone easier on you. I promise I won't work you so hard next time."

"No need to get cocky. I won."

"Yeah, but you're an old guy and I wouldn't want…anything to happen to you."

David's concern cut through Rick, not only

because it made him feel old and feeble, but because it was so uncharacteristic of a twenty-year-old. David should have felt as if he had the world by the tail, instead of worrying that every middle-aged man was going to drop dead of a heart attack.

Seeing David's concern made him rethink his recent wish that Kayla wasn't quite so independent these days. If something happened to him, at least he knew she had a life and would be able to make it on her own. She had a successful career in advertising and lived with her boyfriend, whom she adored.

But what about Gabe's youngest son, Aaron? He had so many fatherless years ahead of him. How would he fare?

Unless, of course, Becca remarried. It could happen—she was young, vital, beautiful inside and out. The thought bothered him for some reason.

"Hey, you're not having a stroke or anything, are you?"

"No, just thinking. You don't need to worry about me, kid, I'm as healthy as a horse."

"Yeah, that's what my dad thought." David shrugged. "I'm outta here."

"Hey, I'll give you a rematch next week, same time, same place."

"I might have something going on next week."

Rick watched David stalk toward the locker room. He felt as if he'd been thoroughly written off. Not because of what he'd said or done, but because David was afraid.

BECCA STOOD in line at the grocery store and watched the woman ahead soothe a fussy infant.

Those days seemed very far away and it barely registered that she might be doing something similar in seven months or more.

Becca had come to at least one decision in the past week. She wasn't going to tell anyone she was pregnant until she reached the end of her first trimester. As Dr. Barker had so tactfully explained, her age made this a high-risk pregnancy.

And with all that had been happening in her life, the baby didn't yet seem real. There was none of the anticipation as with her first three pregnancies. Just fatigue, doubt and fear.

Becca avoided watching the woman and child, glad when they left. She quickly paid for her items and headed home.

She barely had the door unlocked when she came face-to-face with Maya.

"There you are. I was worried."

"That's supposed to be my line." It felt good to smile.

"The doctor's office called to schedule a follow-up appointment. What is it you're not telling us? If it requires follow-up, it's serious. Do you have cancer? Arianna's mom had breast cancer and had to go through chemo and everything."

Becca set down her groceries and enfolded her daughter in a hug. "No, absolutely not. It's all good."

"Then why do you have to go back?"

"It's routine, nothing more."

"You're lying."

Becca sighed. "Only through omission. I'd hoped to have a little more time to get used to the idea myself, but you guys deserve to know what's going on. I don't want to worry you. Tell you what, we'll have a family meeting tonight after dinner. But until then, promise not to worry. It's not anything bad."

It *was* a good thing, right? If Gabe had been alive, they would have rejoiced over this surprise pregnancy, just as they'd rejoiced about Aaron. But Gabe wasn't here and her life was in a scary state of flux and she just didn't know…

"Okay, Mom. We're almost grown up, well, except Aaron. We might even be able to help."

"I'm counting on it." Becca quelled her nervousness at the thought of what her children's reactions might be.

Maya seemed satisfied and went to her room to study.

Becca went to the kitchen to put away her purchases and see if Irene needed help.

Irene. How would this news affect her?

The older woman stood in front of the stove, stirring a pot.

Sniffing the air, Becca guessed spaghetti. Her stomach rebelled at the thought of the acidic sauce.

Then she noticed Irene's shoulders shake.

She touched her mother-in-law on the arm. "What can I do to help?"

Irene wiped her eyes. "Nothing, dear. I just seem to be missing Gabe especially today."

Becca hugged her. "I know. I miss him, too. I can only imagine what it must be like for a parent to lose a child." And here she'd been upset because she was *gaining* a child. How could she possibly be sad?

"I'm fine." Irene smiled. "Nothing for you to worry about."

"I'd worry if you didn't occasionally have

a down day. You're so strong and patient with all of us."

"Not so strong. I'm simply trying to help you as much as possible."

"And you do. What smells so good?"

"Spaghetti."

"How about if I set the table?"

"Absolutely."

The bittersweet moment passed and they were doing their best to move forward. She only hoped her news helped, rather than made things worse.

Dinner was a boisterous affair, as if everyone was trying to pretend life was business as usual. But Becca noticed the children avoided glancing at their father's empty chair. Becca could barely face it herself.

"That was a wonderful meal, Irene," she said. "Thank you. You're an absolute treasure."

"You're very welcome, dear."

"Jim, how's your secret project going?"

Her father-in-law's eyes twinkled. "You're not going to trick me into giving anything away. My project is going well, thank you for asking."

"I'd like to call a family meeting after dinner, if you can spare a few minutes."

"For you, always."

"Good. The children can help me clear the

table and load the dishwasher, then we'll meet in the great room."

For the first time, Becca wished she could draw out after-dinner cleanup. But before she knew it, the kitchen counters sparkled, the dishwasher hummed and the children filed into the great room.

She followed, wishing for a reprieve.

Everyone waited expectantly. For once, the kids were quiet instead of all talking at once.

"I…wasn't going to say anything yet, but I didn't want anyone to worry. And you're all going to be affected by this."

She hesitated, knowing that once the words were out, they could never be recalled. "I went to the doctor last week and there are some follow-up tests I need to take."

Irene covered her mouth, her eyes wide.

"I'm fine. Really. They're routine tests for a woman my age."

"Like school tests?" Aaron asked.

"No, like lab tests. The first is an ultrasound to make sure the baby is developing properly and to determine a due date."

"Baby?" they asked in unison.

"Yes. It turns out your father left us one last, very special gift." She smiled, wishing her knees would stop knocking. "I'm pregnant."

CHAPTER SEVEN

BECCA WAITED for a reaction, but didn't receive one. Her children were absolutely silent.

Jim recovered first. "That's, um, great."

Irene followed his lead. "Yes, wonderful, dear."

"Pregnant?" David's face was pale. "So you and Dad, um, before he died…"

"Made love. Yes."

"But you're okay? There's nothing wrong with you?"

"No, nothing's wrong. Isn't this terrific news?" She hoped her voice was appropriately cheery. Truth was, she didn't know how she felt yet.

"I'm gonna be a big brother. Cool." Aaron whooped.

"That means you won't be the baby any-more." Maya patted his arm, apparently antici-pating the end of his rule as indulged youngest child.

"So you can see I'll need your help now more

than ever," Becca told them. "I'm hoping we can all pull together and make a supportive home for this child."

"Absolutely," Irene said, breaking into a smile. "Imagine, a baby. Another part of Gabe lives on."

"That's what I thought."

Maya gave her a hug. "It's great, Mom. We'll do everything we can to help."

Becca blinked back tears. "Thank you."

"Same goes for me." David joined their hug.

Aaron ploughed into the middle. "Me, too. I'm gonna be the best big brother ever."

"I know you will."

Jim and Irene came over and kissed her on the cheek. "Our own miracle baby."

Becca closed her eyes, grateful for the love and support surrounding her. Everything would be okay.

RICK CAME IN off the lot and saw only one rental agent and Becca at the counter trying to serve several customers.

"Where's David?"

"He's not here yet and he's not answering his cell." Becca handed the keys and rental agreement to a couple, smiling brightly and wishing them a good trip.

"We'll have to call someone in. I'll go check the schedule and take care of it."

Becca nodded, frowning.

He was worried, too. It wasn't like David not to show up for work. If he needed a day off, he always arranged a trade with someone.

Rick tried calling David's cell, but it went straight to voice mail. He left a message, then went down the staff list looking for a replacement.

When he was done, he sent one of the agents out to bring around the cars for their customers while he and Becca handled the counter.

A half hour later, the rush was over, a replacement was in and Rick nodded toward his office. "Got a minute, Becca?"

"Yes."

Once they were inside, he closed the door and went behind his desk.

Becca remained standing so he did, too. Uneasiness washed over him. Something was wrong.

"You've been kind of distracted today. And then David blew off his shift. Is anything going on at home?" he asked.

"Things are…difficult."

He waited.

Becca glanced at the door as if she contemplated dashing outside and never coming back.

Then she met his gaze and raised her chin. "I didn't want to tell anyone this news early in case there were complications, but I guess it's unavoidable. I'm pregnant."

Rick felt his jaw drop open and clamped it shut. He sat down abruptly, unable to speak. Of all the problems he'd anticipated, this one hadn't made the list. Mostly because it might involve him in a very personal way. "You're going to have a baby?" he finally managed to say.

She smiled slightly and sat on the edge of the chair, as if she still might feel the need to flee. "Yes, that's generally what being pregnant means."

"When? How? Wow."

"Yeah, wow."

He was vaguely aware that she hadn't answered the most important question. *When.* Her answer could make a world of difference to his life, and quite possibly, his self-respect. Why a pregnancy made the thought of their lovemaking shameful, he didn't know. Maybe because there would be a very tangible result.

"When are you due? I mean, when did you get pregnant? Am I, um, the—"

"Father? No. Gabe and I made love a few days before he died. Unprotected sex. So you're off the hook."

"You're sure?"

"Positive." But she couldn't quite meet his gaze.

Part of him wanted to accept her calculations at face value. But the mature part of him suspected the timing was too close for her to unequivocally say Gabe was the father. Unless of course, she knew something he didn't. He brightened at the thought. "So you and Gabe, were, um, trying for a baby? Charts and…stuff?"

"Not trying. But not *not* trying, either. Definitely no charts."

Great. On the scale of reassurances, that rated pretty close to a zero. "The timing being so close to when you and I, you know, um—" he lowered his voice "—made love, don't you think it's possible—"

"No, it's not possible. This baby is Gabe's."

The firmness of her answer persuaded him to accept it as fact. It wasn't as if he *wanted* to be a father again at this stage of his life. "We *did* use protection."

"Yes, we did. So we don't need to even go down that road. The baby is Gabe's last gift to me."

Put that way, how could he protest? Part of him was seriously relieved to have dodged that bullet. Heck, *all* of him was seriously relieved.

But what would that mean for Becca? Another child to raise without a father. Though she put on a brave face, the prospect had to be pretty damn scary. And that meant he still had a responsibility as a friend to help her through this.

He reached across the desk and touched her hand. "Do the kids know?"

"Yes, I told them last night. They were surprised, to say the least, but I think we're all happy. Well, David said he was on board, but now with him not showing for work, I have to wonder if he was upset and just didn't let on."

"I tried calling him on his cell and it went into voice mail. Do you want me to call his friends or anything?"

"No. He's technically an adult. We'll have to talk to him about not showing for his shift just as we would with any other employee. But I appreciate your concern." Her eyes shone with moisture. "It helps, knowing I can depend on you."

Her admission made him feel guilty and protective all at once. Or maybe it was her unshed tears and brave posture. He stood and went around the desk, kneeling next to her. "I'm here for you, Bec. Anything you need, just let me know."

"Thank you." Her voice wavered.

He wanted to hug her, but thought that might not be wise. Instead, he patted her knee.

"It'll be okay."

"Of course it will."

But he suspected she might be one shock away from throwing dishes in the kitchen again.

And he wished there was something, anything, he could do to make things better for her.

BECCA ARRIVED for her ultrasound appointment alone. And thought she'd never missed Gabe more.

She didn't even have the familiarity of her own doctor's office, since the clinic's ultrasound machine was being repaired. The hospital technician was gentle and kind, but that still didn't make up for Gabe's absence.

Did he know about their child? Was he somewhere above, cheering them on? The thought should have reassured her, but it only made her uncomfortable.

Because if Gabe knew about the baby, then it stood to reason that he knew she'd made love with his best friend. Something he could only see as a betrayal. Did hearts break in heaven?

She bit back a moan.

"I know, the gel is pretty cold."

Becca nodded.

Watching the screen, she was surprised not to discern the baby. In her previous pregnancies, she'd been much further along when she'd had an ultrasound and she and Gabe had been thrilled to see their child's face, hands and feet.

But today, she saw nothing. Maybe there was some mistake. Maybe she wasn't pregnant at all.

The technician pointed to a flashing light. "See that?"

Becca nodded.

"One of the things we're looking for today is a heartbeat."

"That's the heart beating?"

"Your doctor will go over the results with you. I can't say any more."

"Thank you. You've been very kind."

Her baby was real. And it had a heartbeat.

Becca smiled, overcome by the wonder of it all. She was having a baby!

RICK HATED to pound on the Smiths' door so early on a Saturday morning, but he was determined to get David back on the racquetball court. Something was going on with the kid and he intended to find out what.

That, and he refused to allow Bill to think his court time was up for grabs.

He waited, then pounded again.

The door opened and Irene stood on the other side, wearing a housecoat, her hair slightly mussed. "Rick, is something wrong?"

"I'm sorry if I woke you. David's supposed to be playing racquetball with me this morning and I thought I'd give him a ride." Particularly after the kid hadn't returned his calls.

"Come in. I think he's still asleep."

Rick sat on the couch and waited.

Aaron staggered downstairs, his hair standing on end.

He did a double take. "What're you doing here?"

"I'm here to pick up David for racquetball."

And to check on Becca.

But he refused to dwell on that fact.

Aaron retrieved the remote and turned on cartoons.

Rick was relieved. He wasn't in the mood for a ten-year-old's version of polite chitchat.

Checking his watch, he wondered what was taking so long.

Rick glanced around the room, noting the portrait of the Smith family, with Gabe a central figure. The picture made him uncomfortable, reminding him he hadn't been the best friend he should have been.

But he could make up for that now by helping Gabe's family. He could keep an eye on David and help Becca through this challenging time.

Liar.

He had more questions than answers about the baby's paternity and he didn't quite know how to handle that. He knew he should leave well enough alone, accept Becca's assertion that the baby was positively Gabe's. But he couldn't.

"I'm sorry, Rick. David was still asleep and I had a hard time waking him." Irene made her way slowly down the stairs.

He winced, realizing that climbing was painful for her. Becca had mentioned she had a bad knee.

"I hate to be such a bother, but I called and he didn't pick up his cell."

"It's no bother. Besides, it'll be good for the boy to be up at a decent hour. From the looks of him, he was out late last night. I'm brewing coffee. Would you like some?"

"No, thank you, I'm good."

As a matter of fact, he wanted to bolt the second David showed. The back of his neck tingled and he felt as if Gabe's eyes were boring into his back.

Fortunately, David staggered down the stairs, carrying his racquet. "Hey, man, couldn't you have found somebody else this morning?"

"I would have if you'd called to let me know you weren't going to make it. I tried your cell this morning but you didn't pick up."

"Because I was asleep."

David's sardonic tone grated on Rick's nerves.

"Well, you're not now, so let's get moving."

Becca appeared at the top of the stairs, yawning. She wore pajama bottoms and a little tank top.

"Rick, what're you doing here?"

"I came to pick up David for racquetball."

Now that Becca was here, he wasn't sure what to say. At the office it was easy because they had business to discuss.

"Sleep well?"

"Yes, I did." Becca smiled, but her face paled. "If you'll excuse me—" She slapped her hand over her mouth, turned and ran back to her room.

Rick looked at David, who shrugged. "Morning sickness, dude. The book says there should be another couple of weeks of that. Maybe a month."

"Oh."

Sufficiently uncomfortable, they both headed toward the door.

"Bye, Mom," David called.

Rick breathed a sigh of relief when he shut the door behind him. Trying to keep up with a kid half his age at a demanding sport seemed easy compared with the vagaries of pregnancy. It was a mystery he didn't understand any better than when his ex-wife was pregnant twenty-three years ago.

The drive to the gym was mostly silent, with David resting his head against the door as if he was sleeping.

"Late night?"

"Uh-huh."

"Anything you want to talk about?"

"No."

Rick cleared his throat. "Because, um, with your dad being gone and all, I want you to know you can always come to me if something's bothering you."

David straightened. "Like my father being dead, my mom being pregnant and me not having a clue what's going on?"

Swallowing hard, Rick said, "Yeah, like that. Nobody anticipated either happening, and yet they did, so we've got to deal with the fallout."

"*You* don't have to deal with anything. It's none of your business. I'm the one who needs to be head of the family now."

"You're right. I'm not family. But your father was my best friend and I know he would want me to look out for you guys. Especially now that your mother's pregnant. And I don't think anyone expects you to be man of the house."

David's eyes flashed. "*I* expect it."

Rick figured he was going to get beaten big-time on the court today. Because it looked as if David would like nothing better than to kick his ass.

CHAPTER EIGHT

BECCA ARRIVED at the office before Rick, which was a first. And she'd even stopped for a latte, rationalizing that the milk offset the caffeine. Then she remembered Rick's Saturday-morning racquetball game.

She settled in at Gabe's desk, wondering if she would always think of it that way. Every time she sat down in his chair, she noticed the family photo he'd proudly displayed. It brought an ache so deep it almost stole her breath away. Valentine's Day had come and gone and before she knew it, her first Easter without Gabe would be here.

Becca was tempted to rest her head on the desk and allow herself the luxury of a good cry. But she'd come close to the edge that day in the garage and she never intended to go there again. Keeping her grief contained was the only defense she had.

Brushing the moisture from her eyes, she straightened her spine and booted up the computer, eventually losing herself in figures. A good thing, because she was behind on the accounts receivable they had yet to delegate, not to mention the preparations for swapping the vehicles.

"Hey, you're here bright and early."

Becca jumped, letting out a squeak of surprise.

She turned, startled to see Rick standing right behind her. "You shouldn't sneak up on me like that."

"I made enough noise to wake the dead. I thought you heard me."

Becca swallowed hard.

"Sorry, poor choice of words. I dropped David off at your house with instructions to shower and get his butt down here. We're going to need him all day."

"He was out late again last night."

"New girlfriend?"

"I wish I knew. He stays pretty private. And since he's technically an adult, I don't press him much."

"But you still worry." Rick's voice was warm.

"Yes, I do. It wasn't as bad when I had Gabe to share the worry. But now, it's just me."

Rick sat on the corner of the desk. "You need your rest now more than ever. Tell you what.

When you're having one of those worry times, pick up the phone and call me."

"Sure, at two in the morning."

"Absolutely. I can always go back to sleep."

"I'm not going to do that."

"Seriously, give me a call. I'll be offended if you don't."

"Okay," she lied. He was being so sweet Becca didn't have the heart to tell him there was no way she'd take him up on his offer. "Thanks."

He pushed off her desk. "Oh, and I thought I'd ask what you wanted to do about the company picnic this year."

Becca closed her eyes and groaned. "I'd forgotten."

"Everyone will understand if we decide not to have it. It was Gabe's baby, after all."

Gabe's baby. Becca touched her stomach.

Rick's gaze followed. "Sorry, another poor choice of words."

"But appropriate. Gabe loved planning the company picnic and I think we should continue the tradition. Maybe have it in his honor."

"Excellent idea. Though I'm not as good at event planning as Gabe, I can run with the idea if you'd like."

"No, I want to do this. As a tribute."

"Are you sure?"

"Positive."

"Okay." He smiled, obviously relieved to have that chore off his plate. "If there's anything I can do to help, let me know."

"Believe me, you'll be the first person I call. After drafting the children, of course."

"Yeah, Gabe usually involved them, too. You want to have it in June, as usual? Will that give you enough time to plan?"

"Yes, three months should be plenty of time."

"I'll put it on my calendar. I better get busy." He went to his own office.

Becca realized she was humming. The thought of planning the picnic lifted her spirits. It was such a small thing, but after the past couple of months, a very welcome relief.

BECCA SAT DOWN at the table, relieved to have the long day over. When Gabe was alive, there had been a division of labor that whittled down the considerable family obligations to a manageable size. She knew the van was overdue for an oil change, but she couldn't seem to fit it into her schedule. Thank goodness she had Gabe's parents pitching in where they could.

"The food looks wonderful, Irene. You're one in a million."

"Nothing special, just meat loaf."

"But you don't realize what a help it is to know I don't have to worry about cooking."

"Yeah, and Grandma makes better mashed potatoes," said Aaron. "Yours come out of a box."

Becca would have been slightly offended if she weren't so grateful for the help.

"Where's Maya?" she asked.

"I called her." Irene rose.

"I'll go." Becca placed her napkin on the table. She'd barely had time to talk to her daughter lately. Whatever happened to the long, heart-to-heart chats they'd shared? Her once-open daughter had changed to a guarded teen.

She knocked on Maya's bedroom door, then entered.

Maya sprawled across the bed, talking on her cell phone. She giggled and ignored Becca.

"Dinner."

The girl raised her forefinger to indicate one minute. Or it could have been one hour for all Becca knew.

"Now."

Sighing heavily, Maya said, "I've got to go." She listened intently. "I love you, too. Bye."

Becca resisted the urge to roll her eyes. Maya and her friends lobbed the *L* word around as if it were run-of-the-mill. But something in her daughter's expression told her this wasn't one of her friends.

"Who is he?"

"Why do you think it's a guy?"

"Because you don't get that goofy look on your face for just anyone."

"Mom, you are so lame."

"Didn't you hear Grandma call you for dinner?"

"No." She couldn't quite meet Becca's gaze.

Of all her children, Maya was the worst liar. A fact that made her exceedingly grateful at the moment.

"Next time, make sure you leave your door open so you can hear."

"A little privacy would be nice." Maya flounced out of the room.

"And if you're dating, I want to meet him," Becca called after her daughter, following her out.

"We just hang around the same group of friends."

"Next time you hang around together, I want to meet him."

"Can't you just trust me?"

Becca wanted to say something wise and insightful that would smooth things over. Instead, she let fatigue take hold and said exactly what she was thinking. "You're a sixteen-year-old girl. I trust you, but I don't automatically buy every word that comes out of your mouth."

"I can't believe you don't trust me." Maya stomped down the stairs.

Becca figured she could kiss goodbye the Mother of the Year Award. Shrugging, she joined her family.

Once dinner was over, and the dishes had been cleared and she'd helped Aaron with his homework, Becca felt unaccountably restless. She went for a walk around the block, but that didn't help, either.

She needed adult conversation with someone not related to her by birth or marriage.

When she returned, she went upstairs to her room, intent on changing into her pajamas.

She eyed the phone.

Rick had said she could call. But that had been if she was worried about David being out too late. She couldn't call him every time she felt lonely or scared.

Evenings were always the hardest for Becca because they seemed to stretch out forever, giving her too much time to think. Too much time to miss Gabe and the united-parenting front they'd once provided. Now, it was just Becca on her own, feeling as if she might make a horrible mistake. What would Gabe have done about Maya's new boyfriend? Probably greeted the kid at the door with a baseball bat and a few joking remarks about being good to his princess.

Somehow Becca didn't think it would have the same effect coming from her.

She needed a man's perspective, a father's perspective.

Eyeing the phone again, she wondered if she was simply looking for an excuse to call Rick. They spent so much time at work together, she didn't expect to miss his presence in her off time. But she did. Their shared history meant they could communicate in a shorthand of sorts. Long explanations weren't necessary, which was a total relief. Rick accepted her for exactly who she was—a middle-aged woman trying to hold it together after too many surprising twists in the road.

As the father of a grown daughter, he was the logical choice for her to call for advice. Decision made, she picked up the handset and punched in his number.

"Hi, Rick, it's Becca."

"Becca, is something wrong?"

"No. Yes. I don't know. I just needed to hear another adult voice. And I need some advice."

His chuckle warmed her. "Though my ex-wife might disagree, I'm pretty sure I qualify as an adult."

"I know for a fact Valerie wouldn't think any such thing."

"You caught me. Valerie is probably the most civilized ex on the planet."

"Second only to you."

"I try. What's up?"

"I think Maya has a boyfriend."

"She's sixteen, right? If I remember correctly, having a boyfriend at that age is fairly normal."

"I'm just afraid she might be…vulnerable right now. Might miss her father so much that she'll do something she wouldn't normally do."

"Have you talked to her about it?"

"Only briefly. And she went into the 'you don't trust me' bit."

"I'd say just keep an eye on her. Easier said than done these days, I know."

"That's the truth." She smiled, wondering why it took a fresh eye to make things seem normal and inconsequential. Probably because her whole sense of normality had been turned upside down recently.

"Have you had any ideas about the company picnic?" he asked, changing the subject.

"As a matter of fact, I have. I wanted to stick with tradition at first, but now I'm thinking it might be a good idea to do something totally different this year. We don't want to turn the picnic into a second wake."

"No, we wouldn't want that."

Becca blushed when she remembered how the last wake had ended. She wondered if he was thinking the same thing.

There was an uncomfortable silence.

Becca said, "Well, anyway, I'll work up a couple ideas this week. I better go. Thanks for being my voice of reason."

"Any time. And I mean *any* time."

"Thanks, Rick. You're a good friend." Smiling, she replaced the handset, thinking she was extremely lucky that their friendship had survived the night of the wake relatively unscathed.

RICK EYED BECCA as they walked down a path protected by birch trees at the historic garden. "You've researched quite a few places for the picnic the past couple weeks. This one must be special."

"I think it might be just what we're looking for."

They walked in silence for a few moments. He liked the peacefulness of the place. Though, on a Monday morning, he supposed it was quieter than on the weekends.

Glancing sideways, he said, "You look like you're feeling better these days."

Becca smiled. "I am. The morning sickness vanished as quickly as it came. Earlier than with any of my other children. Then, I was sick the entire first trimester. I'm only about eleven weeks now."

"Either it's the warmer weather of spring or pregnancy seems to agree with you. You've got kind of a…glow."

"Gabe always said the same thing."

They both fell silent. Walking through the gardens, Rick tried to pinpoint his unease. "I wish things could be different for you, Becca. You shouldn't have to work and worry so much."

She shielded her eyes from the sun. "I wish they were different, too."

"Pregnancy should be a happy time."

Her shoulder bumped his as they navigated the narrow path. He'd grown to enjoy the quiet times they had to talk together without business interfering. Her call the other night had pleased him more than he would have imagined. He'd gone to sleep remembering the warmth of her voice as she'd confided her fears. Then he'd dreamed of her, too. Surprisingly, the dream was not a replay of their lovemaking, but a weird sequence where he was trying to protect her from a pack of wolves.

She glanced sideways at him. "I have flashes of joy followed by abject terror. I've never been a single mom before. I've never anticipated the birth of a child without Gabe there to cheer me on."

"I know."

"Don't get me wrong, Irene and Jim have been wonderful. I think they're more excited about this baby than I am. But it's…not the same."

"I imagine it takes their mind off their grief. Whereas you have a whole host of practical details to deal with." And a secret that could wreak havoc if her instincts proved to be wrong. But who could prove her wrong? He was the only one who knew what had happened.

"There are things I have to worry about that weren't an issue with my other pregnancies. Since I'm older, there's more of a chance the baby might turn out to have special needs."

Rick stopped, touching her arm. "Is that what the doctor said?"

"She said the probability of certain birth defects goes up with the mother's age. She suggested amniocentesis."

"That's the test with the needle?"

She nodded.

"They can check for other things with that, too, can't they? Like paternity?"

Becca turned and resumed walking. He thought for a moment she would ignore his question.

"Yes, they can. But I told him I didn't want the test."

"Why? It would answer any residual questions. I know it would set my mind at ease."

"There is an increased risk of miscarriage after amnio. I'm not endangering this child to put your mind at ease. And I'm not going to endanger it to find out whether it has birth defects. With all my heart, I want a healthy baby. But if there's something wrong…I guess I'll handle it somehow."

Rick looked up at the sky, hoping for instant wisdom. When it didn't come, he opted for honesty. "Bec, I'll try to support you in whatever you decide. But I will probably always wonder if—"

Becca stopped. Her voice was tense when she said, "It's *not* yours. Don't you understand? I can't handle the thought of having betrayed my husband that way, conceiving a child on the same day he was buried. I can't handle the thought of what it would do to my family—I have to protect what little peace we have left. Besides, the circumstances almost guarantee Gabe was the father. So why borrow trouble?"

Rick's heart contracted at her absolute certainty, as well as the stark reality of her situation. *Her* situation, not his. Because she carried Gabe's baby, not his. He had to condition himself to think of the child that way. Because if he didn't, the gray areas would make him crazy.

He touched her cheek. "Okay, Bec. I understand. I won't mention it again."

"Thank you."

They resumed walking.

A few minutes later, Becca pointed at the sky. "Look at that bird. Isn't it beautiful?"

"Yes, it is."

And so are you.

"And a good way to ease a tense moment," he added.

Becca tilted her head, smiling, as if willing him to recapture their easy friendship. "It *is* a beautiful bird, though."

Rick noticed the way her eyes crinkled at the corners. She was such a warm person—that's what he'd always liked about her.

He made the effort to switch gears. "Where would we set up the picnic?"

"Over this way." She grasped his hand and he followed. "There's a pond and a meadow area."

Threading his fingers through hers seemed like the natural thing to do.

Becca hesitated, then squeezed his hand. "Thanks for coming with me today. I value your opinion. And the fact that you know the worst about me makes it easy to be myself with you."

"If that's a compliment, then I'm honored."

"Oh, it's a huge compliment. People treat me differently now that Gabe's gone. Even the people who don't know I'm pregnant. It's as if I'm an oddity and they can't quite figure out how to categorize me."

"Part of that's because you've become single after being part of a couple for so long. It's the same when you get divorced. I'd like to say it will get better, but that doesn't always happen. Some married folks are uncomfortable having single friends around. It's almost as if they think divorce is contagious. You and Gabe never made me feel that way."

"I'm glad." She disengaged her hand, but linked her arm through his. "You're right, that's exactly how it is. As if being widowed is contagious. And then there have been a few odd reactions. An old high-school friend of Gabe's hit on me a couple days after Gabe died. And a friend at the hair salon insists I need to sign up for online dating."

Rick stopped to face her, brushing her hair from her forehead. "You'll have plenty of time for that later."

"Maybe something to distract me from colic, ear infections and teething?"

"I see what you mean." He walked a few steps, picked up a stone and tossed it in the pond.

"I'm not sure I'll ever be ready to date again. Gabe was my world. I'd counted on our growing old together. I'm not sure where Gabe's dreams ended and mine began. Does that sound crazy?"

Rick felt a pang of pure envy. He'd always thought Gabe was about the luckiest man on the planet, but he'd been such a good friend, Rick couldn't hold it against him.

He cleared his throat. "It sounds like you were fortunate to have the kind of marriage most people only dream about. And it will be all the harder for you to let go."

That's where Gabe was fortunate even in death. He would always be loved and remembered. Becca would always mourn the huge hole left in her life. And any man she got involved with would come a distant second.

CHAPTER NINE

BECCA USED the straightening iron on Kim Anderson's blond locks, artfully highlighted by Becca. She was one of Becca's best customers and worked in the loan office next door to the rental agency.

"Something's different about you," Kim commented. "Have you done something to your hair?"

"Nothing new."

"You seem refreshed. I hate to say it, but right after Gabe died, you looked so fragile. Now you look…robust."

Laughing, Becca said, "You can go ahead and say it. I've gained weight."

"Yes, but in the best possible way." Kim stared at Becca's chest and her eyes widened. "You had your boobs done," she squealed.

"Shh. No, I didn't. I've gained weight and a lot of it has settled in that area."

Kim pouted playfully. "I sure wish some

would settle that way for me. It all goes to my butt."

Becca tactfully redirected Kim's attention. "I've seen the way Neil looks at you. He loves your butt just the way it is."

"Yes, he does. He's a keeper. Did I tell you he's taking me to the Caribbean for our fifth wedding anniversary?"

"No, you didn't. Dish, woman, dish." Becca breathed a sigh of relief as Kim launched into their travel details.

Becca knew she wouldn't be able to fend off these innocent inquiries much longer. She was fortunate she'd always stayed relatively small when carrying her children. That fact, along with empire waistlines, was her saving grace.

But very soon, she would have to announce her pregnancy and face all the whispered speculation. It was something she could have handled with some semblance of grace if only she hadn't seduced Rick. As it was, she still felt horrible about that. The question was, could she hide her guilty conscience?

RICK GLANCED at the bedside phone. Maybe Becca would call tonight. He'd grown accustomed to their late-night conversations.

Taking matters into his own hands, he picked up the phone and dialed.

Becca picked up on the first ring. "Maya, I hope you have a good explanation."

"Becca, it's Rick."

"Oh, Rick, I'm sorry. Maya's out past curfew and her phone goes straight into voice mail. When the display said Unknown Number, I figured she was using someone else's phone."

Rick didn't like the note of worry in her voice. "When was her curfew?"

"Ten o'clock on a school night. It's almost eleven."

"Maybe she lost track of time."

"The neighborhood branch library closed at ten. She would have been home by now even if she left at closing."

"Who was she with? Maybe you could call her friend."

"She's with her new boyfriend and I don't have his cell number. I'm getting nervous. This isn't like Maya. What if she's hurt or lying in a hospital somewhere?"

"Tell you what. I'll swing by the library and make sure she isn't talking in the parking lot. Kayla used to do things like that. Kids don't understand how much we worry."

"This isn't your problem. Besides, I'm sure she'll be walking through the door any minute."

"You're not sure of that at all, otherwise you wouldn't be worried."

"Rick, you've done so much for me already. I don't feel comfortable with you going out in the middle of—"

"I offered because it's no big deal. Do me a favor and just accept help when it's offered."

Becca hesitated. "Since you put it that way, thank you. You're a lifesaver."

"I'll give you a call when I get to the library."

"Okay."

Rick clicked off his phone and threw on a pair of pants and a shirt. Pulling on shoes, he was out the door in a couple of minutes.

"Inconsiderate kids," he muttered. Maya should know better than to worry Becca right now.

A few minutes later, he swung into the library parking lot.

It was empty.

He got out and walked to the front doors, just to make sure Maya wasn't around.

Nobody.

Walking toward the back, he eyed the dark lawn and looming shrubbery, perfect hiding places for someone with a violent agenda. He couldn't begin to imagine a sixteen-year-old girl venturing out here in the dark. Unless of course she was seeking privacy with a boyfriend.

Or had been taken unwillingly.

It was obvious Becca's paranoia had rubbed off on him. He thought about calling her to see if there was anywhere else he should check, but he was afraid to give her the news over the phone.

Instead, he drove to her house, where the porch light burned brightly.

Becca opened the door before he could knock. "She's not with you?"

"No. I was hoping she'd returned home."

"No." Becca's face was pale.

"Is there anywhere else you'd like me to check?"

"I don't know where this boy lives. That's silly, isn't it? I should have all this information before I let a boy date my daughter."

"How about when he picked her up?"

"She met him at the library." Becca folded her arms over her chest. "I've been way too lax. I guess I've been more distracted than I realized."

"Don't be so hard on yourself. It's not like you haven't had anything going on. Want some company while you wait?"

"I'd love it. Come in."

Rick stepped inside, following her to the great room. He had to wonder at his own motives. He suspected the promise of spending time alone with Becca drew him nearly as much as concern for Maya.

"Would you like coffee?"

"No, thanks. You said this wasn't like her?"

"She used to be very good about curfew. But that was when Gabe was here and she didn't have a boyfriend yet."

"I'm sure it will turn out to be nothing. But I understand how nerve-racking it is for you. I've had a few of those nights myself."

"If Gabe were here, none of this would be happening. I feel like I'm failing my family. There just doesn't seem to be enough of me to go around."

He wrapped his arm around her. "I doubt Gabe would have an easier time dealing with Maya's dating. But there would be two of you and it's usually easier when there's someone to share the worry."

"I guess I'd better get used to it then. I've got to get Aaron through his teens, then the baby through all the milestones." Her voice quavered.

"Aw, Becca, it'll be all right. You have so many people who love you and will watch out for you guys. And I'm at the top of the list."

Uh-oh. Professing love was going a bit overboard. But he'd meant as a friend.

And that's how she accepted his statement, because she nodded and wiped her eyes.

"I know. I'm incredibly blessed to have Irene and Jim. And you."

He studied her upturned face and wondered what the hell was happening to him. He admired her tenacity and compassion, but the desire to kiss her had more to do with memories of how warm and urgent her kisses had been the night of the wake.

Shaking his head, Rick reminded himself of all the reasons he couldn't get involved romantically with Becca, the first being the complex paternity issues of her pregnancy. The second was the scary responsibility of being a middle-aged parent.

His days of raising small children were past. When he got involved again, he hoped it would be with a woman who had the freedom to travel. One who would encourage him to step away from his stable life and explore new things.

He knew from experience that babies thrived on stability.

Clearing his throat, he said, "Maybe the new baby will be a boy. I hate to say it, but there's less to worry about with boys than girls once they hit their teens."

Becca smoothed her oversize shirt, briefly resting her hand on her stomach. "I don't care what it is as long as it's healthy…"

BECCA FELT RICK stiffen beside her. He must have heard the door, too.

She jumped up and went into the entryway, where Maya swayed. Relief warred with concern. "Honey, are you all right?"

"Sure." Maya turned and stumbled toward the stairs.

The smell of alcohol hit Becca, nauseating her.

"You've been drinking again."

Maya started to climb the stairs, but must have realized it required more dexterity than she had at the moment. She sat on the bottom stair, blinking up at her mother.

"No, I…went to the library."

"I want the truth." Becca grasped her chin. "You're out way past curfew and reek of beer."

Maya's bravado crumpled. "I'm sorry, Mom," she whimpered. "It was awful. I went to the library, really I did. But Greg said there was a party, and if we studied really quick we could go and you would never know."

Becca longed to smooth back Maya's dark brown hair. But she had to stay strong. "Apparently he was wrong."

"I had a few beers when we got there... I didn't think it would hurt anything. And everyone says I need to lighten up, that I take everything too seriously..."

"Who says that?"

"Greg."

Becca could have gladly strangled the boy.

"Is he out in the car? I hope he wasn't drinking and driving." The restrained anger in Rick's voice surprised her. And made her very grateful to have him for a friend.

"No, he dropped me off at the curb and left. He only had one beer." Maya crossed her arms over her knees and rested her head, sobbing quietly.

Becca exchanged a glance with Rick. He tilted his head toward the door, as if asking if he should leave.

Shaking her head slightly, she sat on the step next to Maya and slipped an arm around her shoulder. "It's okay, sweetie. You're home and everything will be okay. Tell me what else happened."

"We...made out in the car...and he wouldn't stop...and I pushed him away. He got mad and brought me home."

"You're very sure that's all that happened?"

"Y-yes."

"Because if he forced you to have sex, you might need medical attention."

Maya raised her head, a trace of panic in her voice. "No. We didn't have sex."

Becca lowered her voice to a soothing tone. "Sometimes things happen that we don't intend to happen. Our emotions get out of control, and before we know it, we've done something we regret." She forced herself to concentrate on her daughter, not think about her own situation. "That can be especially true when alcohol or drugs are involved. I want you to know I love you no matter what. There's never anything so bad we can't work through it together. If you tell me you didn't have sex, I'll believe you. But if you did have sex, consensual or not, please tell me now so I can help."

Maya leaned close and rested her head on Becca's shoulder, sobbing. "N-no. We didn't have sex. But I was…scared."

Rick made a noise low in his throat.

His gaze connected with Becca's and she suspected he would protect Maya as if she were his own child. The knowledge reassured her in a way she chose not to examine.

Becca stroked Maya's hair as if she were a little girl. "Sometimes things between a man and a woman can get scary if you choose someone who isn't worthy of your trust." She tipped up Maya's chin. "I think maybe this Greg wasn't worthy of your trust."

"He wasn't." Maya flung herself into Becca's arms.

Rubbing her daughter's back, Becca murmured soothing words.

"I better get going," Rick said. "Now that I know Maya's safe."

"Thank you. I don't know what I would have done without you."

Rick touched her shoulder. "See you tomorrow." And he was gone.

When Maya calmed, Becca offered advice in the gentlest way possible. "When you choose a man to love, choose wisely. Don't throw away your virginity on just anyone."

"Oh, Mom, it's not like Dad was your one and only." Her eyes widened. "Was he?"

Becca hesitated. "Yes, that's exactly what I'm telling you. Your father was my first, and I was true to him every day of his life."

The lie of omission made Becca sick at heart. She hoped her daughter never discovered her hypocrisy. But her greatest wish was for Maya to find the kind of happiness and total trust she'd shared with Gabe.

IT WAS AFTER MIDNIGHT when Rick got home, but he decided to go for a run anyway.

His mind raced ahead while his feet pounded the pavement. Losing himself in the rhythm, he felt the tension seep away.

Maya's pain and confusion had touched him more than he could have anticipated. But he'd actually *felt* Becca's pain bone deep. The pain of a parent unable to protect a child. A parent in the unenviable position of preparing her child for the harsher realities of life.

It wasn't his problem.

His days of waiting up with his heart in his throat were gone. Kayla was past that stage, now a beautiful, intelligent young woman with her whole life ahead of her. And Maya would reach that stage, too. But Becca would probably go to hell and back before it happened.

And as if that weren't enough, she would soon have an infant. Lack of sleep from the demands of a baby and lack of sleep from worrying about teenagers. What exactly would be left of Becca when this was over?

And was any of it his responsibility?

The timing of the pregnancy nagged at him,

even though he'd promised not to discuss it with Becca. Granted, it was highly unlikely the child was his. But there *was* a slim chance. Condoms didn't guarantee one hundred percent protection even during the best of circumstances. And the failure rate went up if they weren't applied correctly.

So what should he do?

What should he do? His feet pounded out each word. Unfortunately, no answer came.

CHAPTER TEN

BECCA SAT DOWN in Dr. Barker's office, waiting for her to finish her phone call.

The doctor replaced the handset. "I have the results from your second ultrasound. Purely to err on the side of caution when the patient is your age."

Becca nodded. "Was everything okay?"

"Everything looks good so far. The fetus appears to be developing normally and we were able to estimate your due date." She gave Becca the date. "A fall baby."

"Yes," she murmured. "I'm so glad everything is fine."

"Do you have any questions?"

"No. I'm sure I may have some later."

"You've been through all this before, but as I told you, the risks increase with age. If you have any concerns, please call us. And you can set up a follow-up appointment on your way out."

"Thank you, Dr. Barker."

Becca managed to walk out of the office and to her car at a sedate pace. She managed not to speed or break any traffic laws on the way home. And when she slipped in the front door, she was able to evade Irene and head straight to her room, where she consulted a calendar.

"Damn."

Calculating backward, she realized the date of conception fell right between the last time she'd made love with Gabe and the day of the wake, when she'd seduced Rick. Which meant she couldn't confirm the baby was Gabe's.

RICK WENT BY Becca's desk. "Hey, did you get everything worked out the other night?"

She glanced up and smiled, but her eyes were shadowed. "I think so. I didn't get much sleep, though."

"That's not good for you."

"No, but it won't kill me, either. When my body's had enough I'll simply have an uncontrollable urge for a nap. So if I disappear for a half hour or so, you'll probably find me in the supply closet."

"Good to know. I was wondering if you'd like to go to lunch? There are some marketing ideas I'd like to run by you."

Liar.

Truth was, he would have liked to take the ball and run with his plans without consulting anyone else. He simply wanted to spend time with her and make sure everything was okay. "How about the burger place around the corner? You look like you could use a cheese-burger."

Becca crossed her arms and laughed. "And what look is that? No, don't tell me, I don't want to know. You are positively psychic— I've been craving a greasy bacon cheeseburger all morning."

"Let's go."

They took Rick's SUV, and since it was early, they beat the lunch rush.

They ordered at the counter, and when their number was called, added condiments them-selves. Rick was amused to see Becca pile on everything, including jalapeños.

"I guess the morning sickness really has passed."

She grinned. "This baby has the appetite of a lumberjack. And he's not picky about what he eats, as long as it's greasy, salty and loaded with calories."

They found a table and ate in silence for a few minutes. Rick could almost see the color return to Becca's cheeks. He reached across and squeezed her hand. "You need to take care of yourself."

"I do."

"All the stress isn't good for you. What was Maya thinking?"

"She wasn't, that was the problem." Becca wiped her mouth with her napkin. "But the good thing is that she's decided not to date Greg anymore."

"That seemed like a no-brainer." He held up his hand. "No, you don't even have to say it. I remember that logic and a girl's heart are often totally unrelated."

"I'm grateful the incident gave me a chance to have a talk with her about her choices. But it shook me, too. Maya has always been my levelheaded one. Schoolwork and her close friends came first. She was never boy crazy or anything."

"You think her sudden interest might be the result of Gabe's death? Maybe she's looking to replace his affection?"

"Interesting theory. Very perceptive."

"Hey, I have my deep moments," he protested.

"I guess maybe I didn't see those much with Gabe around. You guys were too busy doing the guy thing."

"You forget, I was the minority when I was married. With one wife and one daughter, women ruled my house. Even the dog was female."

"Trixie. I remember her. A bichon, wasn't she?"

"Yes. Valerie got custody of her in the divorce."

"You're joking, right?"

He nodded. "Yeah. It just seemed the right thing to do. I'd like to get another dog but I'm not home very much and it doesn't seem fair."

"How about a cat?"

"I'm not much of a cat person."

Becca laughed. "It's not something you get to decide. Once a cat claims you, you're theirs whether you like it or not. Our tortie, Hazel, found us. Came right up to the door and meowed until we let her in. I made the kids put up posters, but her owner never came forward. And as thin as she was, I think she'd been on her own for a while."

"Fortunately, no cat has chosen me."

"Yet." Becca popped a french fry in her mouth, mischief lurking in her eyes.

"Don't be getting any ideas about dropping a kitten on my doorstep, either."

"I wouldn't do something like that, much as

I might be tempted." She sipped her soda. "Now, what kind of marketing plans did you want to talk about?"

They were deep in discussion when Rick looked up to see a tableful of women watching them intently. There was a whispered conversation, then more staring.

One of the women stood and approached their table.

"Becca, how are you?"

"Good, Kim. How's the cut working out?"

The woman ran her hand through her blond hair. Rick supposed it was great, but he liked Becca's simpler style better.

"Perfect, as usual. You're the best, Becca. And this is?" She glanced at Rick, extending her hand.

"Kim, this is Rick Jensen, my partner at the rental agency. Rick, this is Kim, one of my best customers."

He shook her hand.

Kim raised an eyebrow and smiled. "I'd better get back to my table, but I just wanted to say hello."

"See you later."

"Was she looking at my midsection or am I being paranoid?"

"She might have been sneaking a peek."

"Probably thinking I've really let myself go

since Gabe died. Thank goodness the clothing styles now can be very forgiving."

"I'd be more inclined to think she's a little jealous. You've got that ripe, sexy look."

Becca rolled her eyes. "You're good for my poor ego. I'll owe you in a million ways before this is all over."

"What are friends for?" Though he kept his voice light, Rick wasn't sure how much longer he would be content with his role as her friend. Especially since her repayment remark brought to mind a couple suggestions that bordered on X-rated.

Becca seemed oblivious to his dilemma, more concerned about Kim. "I hope she doesn't suspect I'm pregnant. I wonder what she'll think when she finds out. I wonder what everyone will think."

Rick redirected his errant imagination. "I imagine a lot will depend on your lead. You deserve to be happy about this baby. Don't let anyone ruin that. Hold your head up and know that you have more courage and grace than most women."

"Now you're starting to scare me. Where are all these compliments coming from?"

Rick was tempted to lay his cards on the table and simply confess. But their friendship could be irretrievably broken and he wasn't prepared to risk that, along with the resulting professional suicide if things went wrong.

He settled on giving her a watered-down version. "I've always admired your grace and intelligence, your enthusiasm, the way you make people feel welcome in your home."

"Thank you. That's so nice of you to say. And since you started this conversation, it means I get to share a bit, too."

"What do you mean?"

"When Gabe died, I realized I've always assumed people know how I feel about them. I'm trying not to leave so many things unsaid these days, because, well, we never know when it might be our last. I hope you know how very much I admire you. I've always been impressed with how strong and together you are. I've seen divorce destroy other men, but you seemed to pick yourself up and forge a decent relationship with Valerie and stay an involved father with Kayla. It takes a very secure guy to do that."

Rick was pleased by her assessment. "I guess."

"No, really." She reached across the table and clasped his hand. "And the part I especially appreciate is how you've stood by me through this, without trying to tell me how I should do things. Your support is so important to me."

"Anytime, Becca. Anytime."

Emotional support was easy to offer Becca, but the desire to deepen their relationship was hard to ignore. And he was finding it even harder not to wonder if Becca's baby might be his. And if it was, what would he do?

BECCA ARRIVED HOME from work relatively early that evening. Since it was Irene's bridge-club day, she beat her mother-in-law to the kitchen and started cooking supper. Having the chance to cook was kind of nice for a change.

Jim wandered into the kitchen. "Something smells good. I wondered if Irene was back already."

"Nope, just me."

"That's a treat, especially since you seem to be on the run these days. I hate to see you burn both ends of the candle while you're pregnant. Gabe would have hated it, too."

Becca bit back a sharp response. Gabe hadn't intended to leave her high and dry financially. "Sometimes we just have to do what we have to do."

"I'll be back."

She didn't think too much of his disappearance until he reappeared at her side a few moments later, handing her an envelope. "Irene and I discussed this. We want you to have it."

Swallowing hard, she opened the envelope. "There has to be a thousand dollars in here."

"Fifteen hundred. Our rainy-day account. We decided this was a rainy day. It'll pay a few bills after you buy some pretty maternity clothes."

"I can't accept this, Jim." She extended the envelope, but he shook his head.

"You have to. Or we'll be very upset." He frowned at her, which only made her laugh.

"The grumpy act doesn't work. You're one of the most laid-back people I know. And yet stubborn at the same time. How do you manage that?"

"It's a gift."

"Yes, well, I see where Gabe got it." She grasped his hand in hers. "Thanks. You and Irene mean more to me than you will ever know."

Jim cleared his throat, his eyes bright. "I have a project out in the shop that needs attention."

He was gone before she had a chance to ask him where the kids were.

She checked the whiteboard on the fridge for notes. She'd passed David on her way out of the rental agency earlier, so she knew where he was.

Aaron was at his friend Jonathon's house just down the block.

And Maya was at the library.

Becca tried not to worry as she went back to cooking, putting together the ingredients for taco sauce. Surely Maya wouldn't use the same excuse to go someplace off-limits, with her friends, would she?

She was thinking of calling Maya's cell to check up on her, when the girl walked into the kitchen, her backpack slung over her shoulder.

"Mom, you're home." The surprise in her voice tugged on Becca's heartstrings. She had always prided herself on arranging her work schedule so she could be home most days when the children walked in the door. That hadn't been possible since Gabe died.

"Yes, I left a little early today."

"Are you okay?"

"Of course I'm okay." Becca gave her daughter a hug.

"I've heard a lot of bad stuff can happen when someone your age gets pregnant. Miscarriages and things like that."

"It's certainly something my doctor will watch for. But I feel fine. Really."

Maya pulled out a chair and sat down. "Is it weird being pregnant?"

"In what way?"

"Oh, I don't know, like feeling the baby move inside you?"

"I've only felt twinges so far. But it's a miraculous kind of weird when you do feel it," Becca said, making a mental note to buy a new pregnancy book and remind herself of all the milestones.

"Did you and Dad plan it?"

"No, the baby was an unexpected gift."

The aroma of sautéed onions filled the kitchen.

"It's going to be hard for me to explain to the kids at school. I'm way too old to have a baby brother or sister."

Becca couldn't help but smile at Maya's self-involved concern. "I bet some of your friends will think it's pretty cool. And I'm sure there will be some raised eyebrows among my friends, too."

"What if they think you had a fling right after Dad died?"

Becca dropped the cheese grater with a clatter. The question hit entirely too close to home. Not that she considered what had happened with Rick a fling.

"People will think what they want to," she said. "All I'm concerned about is having a healthy baby. Knowing you kids support me will help in a big way."

Maya came over and touched her arm. "Mom, I support you. I don't know what I'd do if something happened to you…"

Turning, Becca enfolded her in a hug. "Nothing's going to happen to me, baby girl."

Yes, and Gabe had said they'd be together forever.

Becca pushed away the insidious thought, concentrating on her daughter instead. They would get through this. They *had* to get through this.

BECCA LOOKED at her reflection in the full-length mirror. Even after extending the waistline of her pants with a rubber band through the buttonhole, she could barely squeeze into them. And the oversize shirt did nothing to dispel the impression of one overweight, middle-aged woman.

Although it wounded her pride to be thought of that way, it was preferable to being outed as a middle-aged, pregnant woman with no husband.

But soon, nothing would disguise her pregnancy. She'd definitely gone beyond the baby-bump stage.

Becca hurried to the office and beat Rick there for the second Saturday in a row. At least he hadn't shown up at her house this morning. David had made it home at a reasonable hour the night before and apparently set his alarm. Anything to avoid having Rick blast him out of bed, she suspected.

"Hey, I smell coffee," he said a few moments later.

"I still enjoy the aroma, even though I drink very little of it myself these days. I'm careful to follow the doctor's instructions."

"All the more for me." His grin was wicked.

"No need to rub it in. By the way, I'm going to take a long lunch today. I'm doing some shopping."

"Baby stuff already?"

"Maternity clothes. I'm, um, blossoming."

He surveyed her and his eyes widened. Letting out a low whistle, he said, "You sure are."

His words stung. "Thanks a lot."

"I meant it in a good way. You look absolutely beautiful. Perfect."

"Good answer. I can tell you're no stranger to hormonal mood swings."

"You can thank my ex-wife for that. I'm pretty good at take-out runs, too, so if you get any cravings at 2:00 a.m., I'm your man."

Her hormones must have been fluctuating more than she'd thought, because his offer was overly appealing. And not only for food. She'd been craving the closeness of making love with a man. The security of being held in strong arms. And the reassurance of knowing a man found her wildly attractive despite the changes in her body.

She only hoped her wayward thoughts weren't reflected in her eyes. Glancing away, she said, "I'll keep that in mind."

"Hey, I got a surprise last night."

"A good one?"

"Depends on how you look at it. Kayla dropped in for a short visit."

"Wow, that *was* a surprise, wasn't it?"

"Yes. She broke up with her live-in boyfriend. Said she didn't want to be around while he moved out his things today."

"I imagine that would be difficult."

"Yes, but possibly not as hard as it is for me, trying to play host to an adult child. I went to get the paper this morning and she'd already read it, scattering the sections. I finally found the sports page wedged under the couch. Then she borrowed my razor to shave her legs. Do you know what that does to a guy's razor?"

Becca chuckled, gingerly touching his jaw. "Doesn't look like she dulled the blade too badly. No visible war wounds."

"No, but it's annoying all the same. I won't say anything, though, because I know she's hurting. Really thought she loved the guy."

"You think she'll want to move in with you?"

His face paled. "Don't even suggest it. I love my daughter, but it absolutely wouldn't work. Fortunately, I think she said something about rooming with one of her friends."

BECCA MANAGED to find one pair of good maternity jeans at the thrift store. But one pair of jeans did not a wardrobe make. She patted the cash in her purse. She hadn't wanted to dip into Jim and Irene's money for clothes, but it looked as if it would be necessary. She couldn't very well go to work naked.

Decision made, she completed her purchase and went to the cute little maternity boutique a few blocks away. It just happened to be next door to the best barbecue place in town, a bonus for a woman with cravings.

Her stomach growled its approval.

Patting her tummy, she murmured, "First things first, baby."

She could have cried with happiness when she went inside and saw a huge clearance sign. Half an hour later, she had several pairs of pants, seven maternity blouses and a little black knit frock she could dress up or down depending on the occasion.

Becca was humming as she accepted her bags and left the shop, where she almost collided with a woman walking past the door.

"I'm so sorry," Becca said.

The woman turned, eyeing Becca's bounty. When Becca recognized who it was, she didn't bother trying to conceal the small, discreet stork hiding in the store logo on her shopping bag. The display window was a dead giveaway. She only hoped Kim would think her purchase was for a shower.

"Becca, what a nice surprise. I seem to be running into you all over town these days," Kim said. "I'll see you Thursday for my regular appointment."

Becca could have cringed at the woman's superior, I-know-your-secret tone. No doubt about it, an announcement was in order.

CHAPTER ELEVEN

As Rick walked across the parking lot, he could see Becca's smile fade and he wondered what the woman had said to her before she turned and went inside the restaurant where he was headed.

"Becca, wait up," he called.

She turned, her hands full of shopping bags. "Rick."

"Looks like your trip was fruitful. I came to pick up some takeout. Why don't we go ahead and eat since you're here."

She hesitated, glancing over her shoulder.

"Did that woman say something to upset you?"

"It was Kim. She saw me coming out of the maternity boutique. I think she may have put two and two together."

"And you're not ready for the whole world to know yet?"

"No. Besides, I didn't like the speculative look in her eyes. As if there would be some juicy gossip attached to my pregnancy."

He supposed she would be a topic of conversation—*Poor Becca, pregnant and widowed.*

Then understanding dawned. "You're afraid people will think you got pregnant *after* Gabe died."

"I can tell that's what Kim thinks."

Worse yet, some people might go one step further with their speculation, wondering if Becca had been having an affair while Gabe was alive. Which was erroneous, but probably too close to the truth for Becca's peace of mind. It didn't do his peace of mind much good, either. But he had to try to ease her worries.

"You can't let what other people think bother you."

"Easy for you to say."

"Why don't you head back to the office and I'll bring the food to you."

"Thank you." The gratitude in her voice made him smile. "I'm hungry."

He tried not to watch her walk back to her car, because he thought Kim might be eyeing them through the window.

Once inside, he could see Kim at the far side of the restaurant with her back to him. After he ordered enough to feed three people, he returned to the office, finding Becca behind her desk.

"Here you go."

He hesitated. If it had been Gabe, it would have been understood that they'd eat together in one of their offices.

Becca propped her hands on her hips. "You're eating with me, aren't you? I feel enough of a social pariah as it is."

Rick chuckled. "We wouldn't want that."

"Good. Sit."

She unwrapped her sandwich and bit into it, closing her eyes with a sigh. After she'd chewed and swallowed, she said, "This is heavenly."

"One of my favorites."

"How are things going at home?"

"I'm glad Kayla found a friend to stay with. Amazing how one child can wreak havoc in only twenty-four hours. Kayla threw out a stack of sailing magazines and I about came unglued when I found them in the garbage."

"You're used to doing things your own way. I've been part of a couple for so long, I don't know how to handle having space to myself. I still can't bring myself to sleep on Gabe's side of the bed."

"It takes a while."

"I miss waking up next to him, morning breath and all." Her tone was wistful.

For some reason, he didn't want to hear about

her life with Gabe. "You'll develop a new rhythm, a new way of doing things."

"I don't *want* a new rhythm. I want things the way they were. Every morning, I wake up and hope this is all just a bad dream."

Rick didn't know what to say. So he bit into his sandwich and took his time chewing. "I wish I had a solution for you."

"You sound like Gabe. Why do men always feel they have to solve things?"

Shrugging, he said, "It's just the way we're hardwired."

"I won't debate the point. Besides, there was something I wanted to discuss with you. David would like to take on more responsibility over the summer. What do you think?"

"That his actions need to match his words. He recently blew off that Saturday shift we were scrambling to cover."

"He says he's bored, needs more of a challenge. Bottom line, he seems obsessed with stepping into Gabe's shoes."

"I'll give it some thought. I'll be pretty busy with the new shipment of vehicles arriving next week."

"He had some ideas on the types of vehicles we offer. He'd like to see more geared toward people his age. Says we have too many grandma cars."

"Midsize sedans are popular with our demographic. We can only rent so many sports cars."

"Maybe if you explain it to him?"

"I'll try to take him under my wing a little more, how does that sound?"

"I'd appreciate it. He really misses his dad, but he's trying to put on a brave face."

"I know." Rick promised himself he'd be more patient with the kid. As it was, it was taking him more time to teach Becca the ropes, when a part of him wanted to do the job all himself.

"You said sailing magazines? I never knew you were interested in sailing."

"I've always thought it was a cool idea. Someday I'd like to build a sailboat from a kit. Then when I retire, maybe live on the boat down in Florida."

"Wow. I never knew. Gabe never mentioned it."

"It wasn't something we discussed a lot. I've just given the idea more thought lately. Especially since Gabe died. Life's too short not to try some of this stuff while I'm still young enough to enjoy it."

"It sounds like a lovely idea." Her expression was slightly wistful.

"Hey, you can always come sailing with me someday."

"Not for a long time, I'm afraid. Babies and

all their paraphernalia aren't really conducive to sailing."

Rick swallowed hard. "Maybe when the kid is bigger…"

BECCA FELT she owed it to her friends at the salon to make the announcement there first. And, of course, she figured Kim would spread the rumor if she didn't come clean.

She brought in brownies and placed them in the break room, then went to tell Meg, the owner of the salon, whose children were both adults now.

"I brought in brownies for a celebration."

"What're we celebrating?"

"I'm pregnant." Becca could feel her smile grow more fixed with every second.

Finally, Meg grinned and enfolded her in a hug. "That's wonderful, dear. When are you due?"

Becca told her.

"Is it a secret, or is it okay if I make an announcement?"

"Please, announce away."

Meg raised her voice. "Everyone, Becca has some happy news she's allowing me to share."

Becca thought Meg put extra stress on the happy part, but wondered if she was simply being paranoid.

"Becca is pregnant," Meg told her staff. "Isn't that wonderful?"

There was stunned silence.

Then, all at once a rush of congratulations from the other women.

"Thanks, everyone. You're the best." Becca breathed a sigh of relief. One announcement down, one to go.

Her first Wednesday-morning client came in and she washed and set the older lady's hair.

Stylist after stylist came by to offer further congratulations.

Susan, who had started at the salon the same time as Becca, gave her a big hug. "What terrific news. If you need anything, let me know."

"I will. Thanks."

The morning went on in much the same vein until Emily, the youngest staff member, sauntered up. "So is it Gabe's?"

"Of course."

"I hear they freeze dead guys' sperm all the time…" Her eyes were bright with salacious interest.

"I imagine they do," Becca murmured. Raising her chin, she said, "But personally, I wouldn't know." Then she turned her back on the little viper.

Becca tried not to let the insensitive comment

get to her, but it did. She'd never even considered cryogenics as a plausible explanation. Not that she intended to lie. The baby was Gabe's, conceived the good old-fashioned way.

But a whisper of doubt made her want to run from the shop.

She couldn't do this. She wasn't strong enough.

But then Becca reminded herself of the innocent child she'd conceived in love with her husband. This child didn't deserve to hear whispers about the circumstances of its conception. It deserved a mother who was strong and sure, able to quell speculation with the absolute certainty of her heart.

Becca vowed never again to doubt, even for a moment, the miracle that had happened in the last days of Gabe's life.

RICK GLANCED at his watch as he motioned the empty hauler into the lot. It was nearly one o'clock. Where was Becca? He needed her on the desk while he and the staff brought the cars around.

Wednesday mornings she spent at the salon and came in shortly before noon.

A few moments later, he was relieved to see her minivan pull into the lot.

She joined him. "The hauler's here early. I would have rushed over if I'd known. I made my…announcement today at the shop, so my schedule got sidetracked."

"How'd it go?"

Becca rolled her eyes. "Besides Emily asking if I'd had Gabe's sperm frozen?"

"I thought it was just guys who were that direct."

"I'd usually say you were right. Otherwise it went pretty well. Stunned silence at first, followed by a lot of good wishes. It's nice to know everyone's there for me."

Rick touched her arm. "I want you to know I'm there for you, too."

"I appreciate that." But her smile was a bit forced. He could almost feel her drawing away from him. "I figured I'd make the announcement here this afternoon. News travels fast."

"Yes, it does. Maybe after we get the hauler loaded with the outgoing vehicles?"

"Okay. Where do we start?"

"You want to handle the desk while we bring the cars around?"

"And let you have all the fun? Heck, no. Didn't Gabe ever tell you I helped out that time you had the flu?"

"I vaguely remember him saying something."

"I can load with the best of them. Let me put away my purse and we'll get started."

"You're sure you're up to it?"

"I'm pregnant, not injured. I'll be fine."

"Be sure and grab some water. We don't want you getting dehydrated."

"Rick, I'm fine. I appreciate your concern, but it's really not necessary."

Why did he get the impression she was shutting him out?

"I owe it to Gabe to look after you."

"You owed it to Gabe to be a good friend to him while he was alive, which you were. Your debt is paid."

Ouch.

He grasped her arm. "Did something happen?"

"No." She glanced away. "I just don't think it's a good idea for us to be super-close friends right now. People might get the wrong impression."

"About the baby?"

"About…everything."

"I don't like it, Becca. There's absolutely nothing wrong with us being friends."

"I don't want my baby hearing whispers about his parentage."

Rick hesitated. "Okay. I'll back off. But if you need anything, all you have to do is ask."

"I know. Thanks." He saw a hint of pleading in her eyes. If his understanding made things easier for her, then he would give it to her.

"Sure, Bec."

But he still had the feeling he wasn't doing nearly enough.

CHAPTER TWELVE

RICK HUNG BACK and watched Becca drive the first vehicle up the ramps onto the hauler. She was a natural. No hesitation, no slipups. She drove with confidence and it was damn sexy.

Shaking his head, he knew that line of thinking was dangerous.

They loaded the vehicles quickly and methodically, as if they'd been working together for years. Rick brought up the rear with the last car, following right on Becca's tail.

She playfully tapped her brakes and he backed off.

Seemed to be the history of their relationship, such as it was. But she waited to walk into the office with him.

"Did I pass muster?" Her confident smile told him the question was rhetorical.

"You did okay."

"Only okay?"

"You're a natural. Was that what you wanted to hear?"

She grinned. "Yes. I wanted you to admit it after you tried to banish me to the desk. Gabe used to say I must have been a race-car driver in another life."

"But can you unload?"

"It's the same thing in reverse."

"We'll see."

"That sounds like a challenge. I think you're teasing me."

"Don't want you getting too cocky." Recalling their earlier conversation, he resisted the urge to throw his arm over her shoulder as they walked to the office. Instead, he bumped her with his shoulder.

"I have teenagers, remember. That pretty much guarantees humility. They have a habit of knocking me off my high horse."

"Ah, yes, teens, the great equalizer. But then you'll have a baby who will think the universe revolves around you. That should bolster your ego."

"Which reminds me. I'd better make my announcement before the office staff leaves for the day."

"After you." Rick held the door for her. "I can handle the desk."

"I thought I saw David's truck pull in. You can give him the choice, but I can almost guarantee he'd rather be at the desk than witness my announcement. I think it embarrasses him that his ancient mother will be having another baby."

"I'll go check with him."

Sure enough, David was very insistent on covering the desk.

Rick thought it would look odd if he weren't there when Becca made her announcement, so he joined the others.

Becca had called everyone together in the large room that housed the administrative staff.

Rick stood in the doorway, leaning against the jamb as she shared her news.

He was probably the only one who noticed the lines of strain around her mouth as she smiled. This was damn difficult, but she was getting through it.

There was a short silence, then lots of hugs and congratulations.

Becca smiled over at him and mouthed, "Thank you."

He nodded and went to his own office.

This being involved but not being involved was difficult. He'd do it Becca's way for as long as he thought it was helpful. But he wouldn't hesitate to step in if needed. Because his attachment to her was something he was having a hard time controlling. The more he saw her, the more he wanted to be with her. And he had the feeling he wouldn't be able to accept staying in the background of her life for very long.

BECCA WAS SETTING the table to help Irene, when Maya stormed into the kitchen on Thursday.

"Thanks for ruining my life, Mom."

Becca raised an eyebrow. "What have I done now?"

"You just had to tell people you're pregnant. It was all over school today. And everyone's talking about how gross it is that my menopausal mother is pregnant."

"I'm *not* menopausal. If I were, this might not have happened, though it's no guarantee."

"You know what I mean. I'll be seventeen years older than this baby. That's just… warped."

Becca's heart contracted. Why did this have to be so difficult?

"Maybe it's not the norm, but there's nothing wrong with the age difference. I'm sorry it bothers you, though."

"Then there's the other stuff."

Becca kept her voice level when she said, "What other stuff?"

"All sorts of rumors that you were having an affair before Dad died." Maya's lips trembled. "You weren't, were you?"

"No, I certainly was *not*. It hurts to think you would even consider that."

"I'm sorry, Mom. There's just so much going on. Then someone said you were, um, artificially…"

"Inseminated?" Becca sighed. This was getting old already. "I can assure you that was not the case. Try not to let the gossip bother you. It will soon die down and people will find something else to talk about."

"Next year is my senior year. I should be carefree and having fun. Not missing Dad like crazy and having to worry about you and the baby and all that."

Becca stepped closer. She tucked Maya's hair behind her ear, just as she had done when her daughter was a little girl.

"You will have a wonderful senior year. I'll make sure you don't miss a thing. We'll all need to pitch in to help, but I promise you'll have your chance to shine."

"You promise? Because Brittany Major said that since her baby brother was born, her mom and dad make her babysit all the time. She never gets to do anything."

"I won't lie. There will be times when I'll need you to babysit. But I don't intend to turn you into a nanny. This baby is my responsibility. All I ask is a little love and support…. It's kind of scary for me to consider being a mom again. It's been years since I've cared for an infant."

Maya patted her arm. "You'll do fine. You're the best mom ever." She hugged Becca quickly, then danced out of the room.

Becca shook her head at the changeability of her daughter's moods.

Irene came back into the kitchen. "That seemed to turn out well."

"I think the crisis is averted. Probably the first of many."

"If it weren't about the baby, it would be something else."

"I do feel bad, though. She's had an awful lot to assimilate in a short amount of time. First, Gabe, now this."

"So have you, dear."

"Yes, but I'm an adult. The baby is my responsibility."

Irene patted her arm. "We'll do everything we can to help."

"I know that. I couldn't ask for better in-laws. You and Jim have been great."

"Are you going to start wearing some of those pretty maternity clothes now?"

Becca smiled at the thought. "Tomorrow. Oh, how wonderful it will be to put on pants that fit."

"Maybe now that the announcement has been made, you can relax a little. This baby is an absolute gift and you should be able to enjoy your pregnancy instead of worrying about what other people think."

"I hope you're right."

"Now, we've got a few minutes before dinner is ready. Why don't you go lie down."

Becca smothered a yawn. "You know, a catnap sounds pretty good."

RICK KNEW it was a lousy idea, but he dialed Becca's number anyway. So much for hanging back and giving her space. He couldn't seem to help himself.

She picked up on the first ring.

"Hey, it's Rick. I just wanted to make sure you were doing okay. I bet it's been a rough couple of days."

"It has. And Maya's on a date with a new guy. I have to admit, I'm kind of jumpy."

"Hopefully she picked a better guy this time."

"I made sure she brought him in to meet me. None of that calling-her-on-her-cell-phone-from-the-car stuff. I was tempted to answer the door carrying Gabe's baseball bat."

He chuckled. "I'm not sure it would have the same effect coming from you."

"Apparently you've forgotten the power of hormonal surges. I can be downright scary at times."

"It's all coming back to me." He was also remembering the upswing of the hormonal surges, when his ex-wife had been particularly lustful.

No way could he think about that in terms of Becca's pregnancy, because then he'd remember in detail what it had been like to make love with her.

"What should I do if she's late again?" Becca's voice drew him out of his reverie.

"Same thing as last time. You can call me and I'll see what I can do to help."

"I can't keep calling you every time there's a teen crisis in the Smith household. Remember, we're supposed to be putting some distance between us."

"I'm trying to forget."

"You're not making this easy, Rick." Her chuckle told him she wasn't upset.

"I don't know what you're talking about."

"Yes, you do. It's better if I learn to stand on my own two feet. You're really sweet to offer to help, but I need to do this on my own. Besides, you have a life to lead, too, and I'd never forgive myself if I interfered with that."

"I called you tonight, remember? I'm the one interfering."

"No, not interfering. Just caring. There's a difference."

If only she knew.

"So, are we good?"

"Yes." She sighed. "Am I going to live through Maya's teens? Did Kayla ever accuse you of ruining her life?"

"You'll survive. And to answer your last question, yes, she told me that on a daily basis."

"Do they grow out of it?"

"Kayla did. Now she nags me about my diet and cholesterol. I think I liked the complaining better."

"I'm glad somebody's keeping you on your toes. It's only because she cares. I wish I'd nagged Gabe more."

"You had no way of knowing."

"It's just one of a long line of what-ifs."

Rick didn't know what to say. He'd heard people tell her it was simply Gabe's time to go, but that didn't seem to be much comfort.

"Sometimes I wish I hadn't insisted on all those pizza-and-wings stops, too," he said. "I—"

"There's my call waiting. It's Maya. I better go."

"Sure. Talk to ya later."

"Rick?"

"Yeah?"

"Thanks for calling. It helped."

"Anytime. Bye."

CHAPTER THIRTEEN

IT WAS WEDNESDAY, Becca's longest day of the week by far, and she was grateful for her increased energy level. She didn't dare wonder how everything would get done once she was in her third trimester.

But now, the almost superhuman boost of impending motherhood fueled her days. It was as if she was unstoppable. Her ego took a much-needed lift as she ferried children from activity to activity, helped with homework, volunteered in the classroom and still worked two jobs. Because, after her recent conversation with Maya, Becca wanted so badly to show her kids that this baby wouldn't impact their lives in a negative way. The baby would only add more joy to their full schedules.

Rick sauntered in after lunch while she was handling the desk.

"Bob at lunch?"

"Yes."

"We'll rearrange our lunch schedules so you don't have to be on your feet."

"Not a problem yet. I've already come up with a solution for later, though. Bob's going to bring one of those tall stools from the storeroom."

"Good thinking. You've been a real dynamo lately, always one step ahead of me. And you're looking great."

He eyed her new maternity blouse, skimming her curves.

Becca's face warmed. Not because he seemed to have noticed her breasts growing at a phenomenal rate, but that she *wanted* him to notice. Her libido had returned with her energy level and it had the awful habit of distracting her at the most inopportune times.

At night, she had glorious dreams of making love with Gabe. In the morning, she'd reach for him, sure he was alive and well, only to find his side of the bed cold and unmussed. Try as she might, Becca couldn't summon his scent on the pillows anymore.

But what worried her were the other dreams. The ones of Rick, where they started out on the kitchen floor, but ended up in her bedroom. They made slow, sweet, mind-blowing love in the bed she'd shared with Gabe. The guilt the next morning was almost more than she could stand.

"Are you okay?" Rick's voice was full of concern.

"Yes, sorry, just daydreaming."

"You ate lunch, didn't you?"

"Yes. I'm fine. My mind just takes some weird flights of fancy these days." She couldn't quite meet his gaze, afraid he could somehow sense her fantasies.

It was the pregnancy, nothing more. She didn't want to face the possibility that Rick was becoming an important part of her life. Or that her feelings seemed to be subtly changing, until she didn't know where friendship left off and a more complex relationship began.

"Hey, I forgot to tell you. David missed his shift last night. He never called in. Was he sick?"

"I distinctly remember Irene saying he'd left for work. I'll talk to him, though. Maybe there was a mix-up with the schedule."

"That's probably it. Has he been keeping up with his classes?"

"As far as I know. Why?"

"I overheard him talking with one of the rental agents about a party he'd been to. And he was hungover Saturday when I picked him up for our racquetball game."

"I tell myself it's just boys-will-be-boys stuff." Becca's stomach knotted. "But I wonder if there's something more… This is the kind of thing Gabe would have handled."

"Do you want me to talk to him?"

"No." But it was tempting to turn the problem over to his capable hands. She was so unaccustomed to making decisions regarding the children all by herself. "Well, maybe if you can think of a casual way to lead into the conversation with David?"

Becca felt guilty for asking, especially since she'd implored Rick to keep his distance not long ago. Worry about her son kept her from retracting the request.

Rick nodded. "Absolutely. He'll never know we've been discussing him."

"Thank you. It will ease my mind." On impulse, Becca gave him a quick hug.

His expression was unreadable, but he hugged her back and it felt…right. She closed her eyes for a second, savoring the way it felt to be held by a man. Warm, protected…cherished. Startled by a wave of overwhelming tenderness, she released him and backed up a few steps.

"Anyway, thanks." Becca bit her lip, turned and walked away. The reflection in the glass partition showed her he was still watching her.

When the elementary-school principal called

an hour later, her confusing emotions about David's problems and Rick went straight to the back burner. She briefly told Rick where she was going and why, then hurried to her car.

When Becca arrived at the principal's office, her heart lurched at the sight of Aaron, her sweet, sweet baby. His shirt was torn, his hair mussed and his face was smudged with dirt. A bruise appeared to be starting near his right eye.

"Aaron, are you all right?"

He wouldn't look at her. "Yeah."

"Mrs. Smith, please sit down." Principal Potter motioned toward the chair next to her son.

"What happened?"

"Apparently, the boys said some mean things to Aaron and he flew into a rage. Took on all three of them."

"Aaron? Starting a fight?" Becca would have more easily believed the principal if she'd said Aaron had sprouted wings and flown around the playground.

"Yes. One of the boys had a nosebleed and was so upset he had to be sent home."

"I'm sorry." She grasped Aaron's chin. "What's going on?"

"They were talking trash and it made me mad."

"You know better than to resort to fighting."

"Uh-huh." He didn't look contrite, though.

"We've never had an ounce of trouble from Aaron before, and if it were completely up to me, I'd be inclined to be lenient and possibly consider in-school suspension and a meeting with the school counselor. Especially since he's so recently lost his father."

"I didn't *lose* him. He's dead."

"Aaron!"

"Aaron is right." The woman's smile was kind. "Unfortunately in this case, the guidelines are quite clear and I'll have to suspend him from school for three days. He can meet with the counselor upon his return."

Becca swallowed hard. There was no way she could afford to take three days off from either job. Irene and Jim would probably be able to watch Aaron at least part of the time. "I understand. Do I need to collect his work from his teachers?"

"Yes. I'll make sure his assignments are in the front office by noon tomorrow. You can pick them up there."

"Thank you. He'll have plenty of time for his schoolwork, since he'll be grounded for a long, long time."

Becca stood to leave, feeling as if her world was crumbling bit by precious bit.

"I'VE FOUND the perfect location for the company picnic and I want to take you there at lunch. It's kind of a variation of the gardens we saw."

Rick glanced up from the report he'd been reading and smiled. Seeing Becca so enthusiastic warmed his heart. Especially since she'd been worried about Aaron.

"Okay. Why do I get the feeling there's something you're not telling me?"

She grinned. "Because there is. Think you'll be free about noon?"

"For you? Of course."

"Good. I'll go pick up sandwiches and drinks then swing by to get you."

"Okay."

Becca left and he went back to reading his report, though he couldn't give it his entire attention.

When she returned, he slid the report into a file folder and promptly forgot about it.

"Where are you taking me?" he asked, once they were on their way.

"Washington Park."

"Really?"

"Yes, really."

"Isn't it a little…small?"

"I think it's perfect."

How to get his point across without hurting

her feelings? He tried again. "Isn't it kind of… uninspiring?"

"Yes. Like I said, it's perfect."

Rick clamped his mouth shut, determined not to rain on her parade. Becca needed a cause, something to divert her from recent troubles. Something to make her feel in control again. And apparently this project was helping her do that.

When they pulled into the parking lot of the park, he cleared his throat. But he didn't say a word.

"Will you get the drinks?" Becca asked as she grabbed the sack with a deli logo on the side. "I've got the food."

"Sure." He carried their sodas. "Where to?"

"How about that picnic table over there?"

The steel picnic table looked sturdy enough. Rick sat down and unwrapped his sandwich. Glancing around, he noticed the place was deserted. With the unusually warm weather, the lack of playing children was a reflection on the sad state of Washington Park. "Was the water park already booked for the first weekend in June?"

"I didn't ask."

Rick bit into his sandwich, trying to see where Becca was going with this. For the life of him, he couldn't figure it out. "The botanical place you took me to was kinda nice."

"That's where I got the idea. That, and the Topiary Garden in Columbus. I remember my kids were fascinated by the whole *Edward Scissorhands* thing."

"I think I've been there. Tons of greenery and flowers. Where the plants are trimmed to make a scene from one of Seurat's landscape paintings?"

"Yes, that's the one."

Rick gestured toward the sparse, scraggly shrubs and the tired playground equipment. "And what made you think about this place? I don't quite get the connection."

"I'd like to do something different for the picnic this year. The water park will always remind me of Gabe. I think it will be that way for a lot of our employees."

"Yeah, I still remember him going down the Mondo Slide on his stomach."

Becca smiled. "The lifeguard just about had a fit. If I remember correctly, you went headfirst before him. You two were like a couple of kids."

"I don't remember being the instigator." Rick grinned. "But you're probably right about the water park. It wouldn't be the same without Gabe."

"What I'd like to do is combine our picnic

with a little community service. In the morning, we could clean up the grounds, paint, maybe add some new playground equipment purchased by the business. Then, each employee would receive a shrub or small tree to plant in Gabe's memory. I've checked, and if we commit to this, we'll be allowed to place a memorial plaque in Gabe's name."

Rick had a hard time swallowing. Washing his sandwich down with soda, he cleared his throat.

Becca grasped his hand. "What do you think? Would the employees go for something like that? Or am I being selfish, expecting them to do a lot of manual labor? I could still contact the water park."

"No, Becca, it's perfect." So perfect his eyes watered. "I can't think of a better tribute to Gabe and a great day for our employees. We could make it a yearly project. Take the park on as our own community service. Everyone would start to feel as if they had a stake in it."

Beaming, she fairly vibrated with excitement. "That's exactly what I was hoping. Then after the planting ceremony, we'd have a catered picnic, maybe one of those castles for the kids to jump in, face painting, games and prizes. A real celebration."

"You are truly an amazing woman."

What he wouldn't give for her to feel so strongly about him. Rick could have kicked himself for being jealous, but there it was. Even dead, Gabe seemed to have it all. Becca's adoration at the very least.

"Not amazing." Her smile faded. "Just a little lost and trying to find my way home."

His chest tightened at the way her voice trembled. It brought out every protective instinct in his being.

He glanced away, afraid of what might be revealed in his expression. "Sometimes home is closer than you realize."

CHAPTER FOURTEEN

BECCA WAS TOUCHED by Rick's support of her idea. But when they got back to work, he shut himself in his office, making her wonder if she'd misinterpreted his reaction.

He dropped by a half hour later and placed a sheet of paper on her desk.

"Just something I came up with on the fly. I'm sure you'll have more ideas later."

Picking up the paper, Becca could barely believe her eyes. "It's perfect. You've combined the spirit of fun with giving back to the community. And the dedication to Gabe is wonderful. Maybe I could convince Jim to incorporate elements of your design in a memorial plaque he's creating. I bet he'd be thrilled to have it displayed at the park."

"That would be great, but go with whatever you think best. I don't want you to think I'm trying to take over your project. It…fired up my imagination."

Becca grasped his hand. "I'm so glad you liked it. I was afraid it might be a dumb idea."

Bill walked in with damage reports. He glanced at their clasped hands and smiled. Then placed the reports in her in-basket and left without saying a word.

Becca released Rick's hand. "I hope he didn't jump to the wrong conclusion."

Rick shrugged. "Probably not."

Her cell phone rang, keeping Becca from asking Rick what his cryptic statement meant. That Bill probably hadn't jumped to the wrong conclusion? Or that he'd jumped to the right conclusion?

She checked the display. "It's home. Do you mind if I keep this sketch?"

"Not at all. Like I said, it's just a starting point."

"Thanks."

Rick nodded and went to his own office.

Flipping open her cell, she answered while studying Rick's work. It was quite good.

"Mom, I'm bored."

"Aaron, I'd almost forgotten you were home. If you're bored, you only have yourself to blame. Maya is going to pick up your school-work. Then you'll be plenty busy."

"Why can't I watch TV?"

"Because you're grounded."

"How about the computer? That's educational."

"Nope. I left a list of chores on the fridge. You might want to get started."

"But—"

"No buts. Please don't call me while I'm at work unless it's an emergency. And boredom doesn't qualify."

She clicked her phone shut.

The rest of the afternoon flew by. When her phone rang again, she was surprised the call wasn't from home. Aaron had apparently taken her seriously.

Instead, it was one of her salon customers.

"Hello, June. What can I do for you?"

She listened as the woman's tale of woe tumbled out. "Okay, I'll leave the office early and meet you over at the salon in, say, half an hour?"

Clicking her phone shut, Becca gathered files to work on at home tonight and went by Rick's office. He was nowhere to be seen.

She explained to Bill. "You ought to be able to handle the desk alone until David comes in. He should be here any minute now. And Rick's around somewhere…"

"He left a few minutes ago. But I can hold down the fort."

"I appreciate it. My client was near hysteria. Coloring crises wait for no man."

RICK PULLED UP alongside the police cruiser. He got out of his SUV, eyeing the damage to David's pickup as they hooked it to the tow truck.

David stood by the shoulder of the road, talking with the police officer.

The officer handed David his driver's license. "You can go now, if you're sure you don't need medical attention."

"I'm a little sore. No big deal."

"You okay?" Rick asked.

"Yeah, I think so. I'm just kind of freaked out."

"Looks like you got hit pretty hard."

"The guy said he didn't see me stopped at the light. He plowed right into me and pushed me into the car ahead."

"You're sure you don't need to go to the hospital? Maybe you better call your mom. Probably what you should have done in the first place."

"No! Like I said on the phone, she's got enough to worry about already. And now my truck's totaled."

"Do you want me to take you home? I think you're scheduled to work tonight, but—"

"I'll work. Can I drive one of the rentals home after my shift?"

"We'll have to talk that over with your mom."

"Okay." David ran his hand through his hair. "Thanks for coming to get me. I didn't want Mom coming out here and seeing the truck and thinking I'd almost gotten killed or something."

"Probably good thinking. In her condition, she doesn't need any big shocks. You want anything from your truck?"

"Nah." David snapped his fingers. "Wait a minute, I need something from the glove box."

He went to the passenger side and opened the door. Leaning inside, he pocketed something small.

From the way David glanced over his shoulder, Rick assumed he didn't want anyone seeing what it was.

Drugs?

Rick hated being so suspicious. But David had been partying a lot lately. Who knew if he used drugs.

Rick resolved to keep a closer eye on him.

WHEN BECCA ROUNDED the corner of their street that night, she thought of only two things: food and a warm, soothing bath.

When she pulled into the driveway, she

slammed on her brakes to avoid the monstrosity blocking the whole drive.

David's truck. Buckled and twisted in such a grotesque manner she knew no one could have survived.

Her heart started pounding. She jumped out of the car and jogged toward the door, sure that police officers were inside, waiting to deliver tragic news.

An awful sense of déjà vu set in.

Becca's legs nearly buckled. She couldn't do this.

Surely God wouldn't be so cruel.

Her fingers shook as she fit her key in the lock. She stepped into the entryway, waiting for the horror to unfold. But there was no one in sight.

The sound of the television came from the direction of the great room.

Slowly, she forced herself to move.

When she rounded the corner, she was surprised at how normal everyone appeared. Irene and Jim sat close together on the couch. Maya slouched in the easy chair, her fingers flying over the keypad of her phone. And Aaron sprawled on the floor.

Aaron jumped up. "Mom!"

Irene glanced up. "Hello, dear. I left a plate for you in the refrigerator."

"I was, um, just talking to Grandma about something and I got sidetracked." Aaron sidled past her.

Then she remembered. "You're grounded," she said, "with no TV."

"I'm sorry, Mom. Really sorry. Please don't add time to my punishment."

"We'll discuss it later."

"Okay. I'll be up in my room." He made a hasty retreat.

"Where's David?"

Irene frowned. "Wasn't he working tonight?"

"Irene, I saw the truck in the driveway. I need to know what happened to him. You don't need to protect me. Just tell me."

"Protect you from what? His truck shouldn't be in the driveway if he's at work…" She pulled the drapes and gasped. "Oh, my lord. I—I don't understand. Jim, come look."

Jim rose stiffly and glanced out the window. He cursed under his breath. "That wasn't there when I came home from the hardware store."

"Where's David? I—I'll call the hospitals." Then the morgue.

"Dear, why don't you call his cell phone first."

Becca felt as if she was losing her last shred of sanity. Her voice was shrill when she said, "Look at his truck. He's been badly hurt or worse and there was some mix-up and they forgot to inform us. Maybe he didn't have any ID."

Irene grasped Becca's arms and squeezed. "Becca. Listen."

The discomfort made her focus.

"We'll call David first. Then the rental agency. If we can't reach him at either place, *then* we'll start to worry."

Becca nodded, numb.

"Do you want me to do it?"

"Yes." Because Becca couldn't function, couldn't move, scarcely even dared to breathe.

Irene picked up the handset from the end table. She punched in the button for David's cell.

It seemed as if she was quiet forever.

"David? This is Grandma. Are you all right?"

"It's David? You're talking to David?" Becca reached for the phone. "David, is that you?"

"Yeah, Mom."

"You're alive? You're okay?"

"How'd you find out about the accident already? I meant to tell you when I got home. I didn't want you to worry."

Becca's knees started to shake. "Your truck is in the driveway. What's left of your truck."

David swore and Becca didn't even correct him.

"They were supposed to take it to the tow yard. I'm okay. Just a little sore."

"But your truck looks totaled."

"It probably is. The air bag went off, so that's what saved me."

Becca tried to say something reassuring, but all that came out were sobs and hiccups.

Irene pried the phone from her hand.

"David, I think you need to come home now so your mother can see for herself that you're fine. She's had quite a scare. It was horrible for her to find out this way."

RICK'S TIRES screeched as he took the corner faster than he should have.

David braced his hand against the dash. "Hey, man, the whole idea is to show my mom I'm alive. We can't do that if I'm killed before we get there."

Rick took a deep breath and eased off the gas. "Sorry. I'm worried about Becca."

"My mom is worried about me and is, like, probably going into labor. You're worried about my mom so you're going to get me killed. There's something seriously screwed up about this whole thing."

"It goes with the territory of…caring. For your friends, for your family," he quickly amended. He didn't want David getting the wrong idea.

Yet his foot pressed on the gas pedal again.

He came to an abrupt stop in front of the Smith home. It took only a glance at the hulk of twisted metal in the driveway for his worry to hit full force. He gestured angrily at the heap as he got out of his car. "This is exactly what we wanted to avoid. What idiot left that here? It was supposed to go to the tow yard."

Rick took the steps in a single leap, with David struggling to keep up.

He rang the doorbell without thinking.

It opened almost immediately. Becca's eyes were wide as she gazed past him. "David."

Her face paled. Her eyelids fluttered.

It seemed as if Rick saw her fall in slow motion. But not slowly enough for him to reach her in time.

CHAPTER FIFTEEN

BECCA OPENED her eyes to see Rick's face close to hers. She smiled.

"You really gave us a scare," he said.

She realized that not only was Rick close, so was David, with the rest of the family hovering behind him. She was lying on the couch.

Reality came flooding back.

"David!"

"I'm all right, Mom. A little sore, but that's about it. The tow company must've made a mistake. I'm sorry, I didn't want to worry you."

"What happened? One minute I was standing there, the next…this." She gestured toward her prone position.

"You fainted, dear," Irene explained. "How do you feel? Any cramping or pain? We might need to call the doctor."

Becca concentrated. Nothing seemed out of the ordinary. "I feel fine. I'm just so relieved to see David in one piece. When I saw your truck, I thought the worst…"

"I know. I'm gonna give that tow truck company a piece of my mind."

Becca gingerly raised herself upright. The room didn't tilt, which was a good sign.

"I feel silly. I've never fainted before."

"You've never been a widow and pregnant at forty-one before, experiencing yet another shock," Irene said.

She winced. "Thanks for reminding me."

"Maybe you're a bit dehydrated. Let me go get you a glass of water. Be sure to stay seated until you're certain you won't faint again."

Rick put a pillow behind her and encouraged her to lean back. "Better?"

"Yes." Becca found Rick's concern very soothing. Almost as if he could protect her from bad things happening. She sorely needed that kind of reassurance, though logically, she understood he couldn't protect her from everything.

Maya knelt next to her. "I'll help Aaron with his homework. You just rest."

Irene returned with a glass of water. "You haven't eaten yet, either. I'll go make a nice turkey sandwich for you." She headed back toward the kitchen.

"No, that's not—"

Rick grasped Becca's hand and squeezed. "Just let her take care of you. It gives her something to do instead of thinking of all she's lost."

Becca closed her eyes for a second. "I didn't even think how this must have affected her. She's so strong, sometimes I forget that she's lost a child, probably the most tragic thing a parent can experience. If it helps, then I'll be a model patient."

"Good."

"But there's no need for all of you to gather round as if I'm on my deathbed. David, why don't you go try to reach our insurance agent to make a report. There may be an automated system."

"Yeah, I didn't think of that."

"And Maya, I'll take you up on your offer to help Aaron with his homework. He's upstairs."

"Sure, Mom. The brat has a ton of homework. They must've wanted to make an example of him for fighting."

"Jim—"

Her father-in-law smiled. "You don't have to tell me when I'm not needed. I'll just wander out to the shop."

When he left, Becca sighed with relief.

Rick sat next to her on the couch. "You really know how to clear a room."

She smiled weakly. "It's a gift. I'm not comfortable with all that attention."

"Yet you didn't chase me off. Why is that?"

"You don't hover. And I don't have to pretend to be strong for you."

He brushed her bangs back. "Bec, you never have to pretend to be strong for me."

The moment seemed to crystallize in time for her. She held his gaze for what seemed like forever, barely aware of leaning toward him.

He bent his head, brushing his lips against hers.

Becca held her breath, not knowing how to react. She wanted to melt into his arms and feel safe and loved. When she didn't move, didn't respond, he drew away.

And just in time, it seemed.

Irene bustled into the room and handed Becca a plate. "Rick, you make sure she eats all of this. She needs to keep her strength up and give that baby plenty of nutrition. That's my grandchild she's carrying, after all."

"Yes, ma'am."

"Are you sure you don't want me to call the doctor?"

"I'm sure. If I notice any cramping or spotting, I'll call Dr. Barker right away."

"Well, then, I have some reading to catch up

on in my room. If you need anything, Becca, let me know."

"Of course. Thanks, Irene."

When she left, Becca was uncomfortably aware of Rick. She felt like a teen left home alone for the first time, sworn to be on her best behavior.

"I don't know what I would have done without Irene. She's been an absolute gem."

"I give you a lot of credit for making it work," Rick said. "There's no way I could have lived under the same roof with my mother-in-law. How come they never moved back into the guesthouse?"

"They were going to after my brother, Royce, recovered from his welding injury. That was nearly three years ago, and somehow they just never got around to it. Gabe and I decided not to push. For some reason, they're wary of staying by themselves. It might have something to do with that fall Jim had a couple years ago. I think it scared both of them. The walkway between the guesthouse and here ices over pretty badly in the winter."

"I guess it's fortunate things turned out the way they did. I mean, can you imagine how difficult it would be—" he glanced around to make sure none of the kids had silently entered the room "—if we hadn't used protection?"

Becca didn't bother to tell him the thought kept her up some nights. She straightened, her back rigid, her voice low when she said, "Well, we did, so it's not a problem."

"I guess not."

But he looked thoughtful.

Oh, no. She could not, would not allow him to go down that road again.

Grasping his hand, she squeezed it tightly. "This baby is my last gift from Gabe. I believe that with every fiber of my being. You promised not to bring it up again. I need you to keep that promise and believe in me."

He hesitated.

"Please tell me you believe I'm right."

"Sure, Becca, I believe," he murmured. "I'm going to leave now. You need to take it easy."

He rose, kissed her on the cheek and left.

Becca stared at her sandwich, but her stomach churned. There was a way to lay all the doubts to rest once the baby was born. But was she brave enough to suggest it?

RICK WAITED for Becca to come in on Monday morning. She'd called to say she had a doctor's appointment purely as a precautionary measure after her fainting episode.

He was relieved when he glanced up from his

computer a few minutes later and she came by his office.

"How'd it go?" he asked.

"Fine. The doctor says I'm fine."

"That's good to hear."

"I was going to call you on Sunday to let you know I hadn't had any more light-headedness, but I…well…wasn't sure if I should."

"Why not?"

"The way you left the other night, I thought you might be angry."

"No, not angry." Just disappointed. For no damn good reason. Or not one he wanted to examine.

He'd gone home and flipped through his nautical catalogs. But even those had failed to hold his interest. He couldn't stop thinking about Becca and all the people affected by her unborn child.

And couldn't seem to shake the feeling he should be doing more. More of what, he wasn't sure. Except his gut seemed to be telling him to get more involved. His head, on the other hand, was telling him to leave well enough alone.

Becca had simplified things to the point where everyone was happy. No need to rock the boat.

"Are you okay?" Becca asked. "You seem… distracted."

"Oh, um, just thinking about the boat kit I might order. Wondering if I could rent a storage locker."

Becca tilted her head. "I'll let you go then. I've got a ton of work to do. And I need to take a couple appointments at the salon this evening."

"That makes for a long day."

"You're telling me. But no longer than the day you put in when the car shipment arrived the other day. I'm sorry I couldn't stay to help."

"You're doing the best you can. I understand."

"I'm trying to pull my weight. I hope I can be more productive this weekend. I'll be in extra early on Saturday."

"Becca, you have nothing to prove to me or anyone else around here. We know how hard you work."

But it was as if he hadn't spoken.

"Oh, and I wanted to let you know I secured the park permits we'll need for the picnic," she said. "Tomorrow, I'm meeting with the man in charge of park landscaping, so we can come up with a cohesive plan. Then I'll need to contact a nursery to find the best deal."

"Sounds like you've got everything under control."

Her smile of relief told him he'd said the right thing.

"Would you consider going with me to meet the landscaper? I'd love a second set of eyes and ears."

"Sure. What time's your appointment?"

"Eleven tomorrow. I can swing by the office about ten-thirty and pick you up."

"Okay. I'll be ready."

Becca went to her office.

Rick tried to turn his attention to his project, but he found himself thinking about Becca and how hard she pushed herself. He only hoped she'd take it a little easier once she felt comfortable in her role as partner.

BECCA SAT nervously behind the wheel. She'd noticed Rick checking her out before she got in the car. "Are you going to say something?"

"About what?" he asked.

Starting the ignition, she maneuvered through the parking lot and exited on Main. "It's the first time I've worn this maternity outfit. You don't like it, do you?"

"I didn't say that."

"You didn't have to. The look on your face said it all."

And it hurt. She'd been excited to get the chance to show off.

"You look beautiful. You were looking a little

pregnant before, but now, you've…well…blossomed even more."

"I'm not a flower. I'm pregnant."

"No, it was a bad analogy. You have this ripe, womanly thing going on."

She glanced sideways at him, noticing his ears turning pink.

"You're embarrassed." Becca couldn't help but laugh. "I don't think I've ever seen you embarrassed before. That makes going from a flower to fruit bearable."

"You don't need to rub it in."

"Why are you so self-conscious all of a sudden?"

"Because you're sexy as hell. There, I've said it. Are you happy?"

Stunned was more like it. And, yes, unaccountably happy.

"You think I'm sexy? Really? Would you say it again? And again?"

"It was hard enough to say the first time," Rick grumbled.

Becca grinned the whole way to the community center where they were to meet the landscaping coordinator.

"Thank you, Rick. You always seem to know the absolute best thing to say to me. I was worried I looked fat and tired, even in my new clothes. You made my day."

She put the car in Park and leaned over and kissed him on the cheek. "And I love you for it."

Her voice came out huskier than she intended. And she hadn't expected Rick to turn and look at her so intently.

And she certainly hadn't expected him to lean close and kiss her. Not his usual respectful kiss on the cheek. No, this was a kiss on the lips, tender, yet full of promise.

She twined her arms around his neck, returning the caress of his lips and tongue. Sighing, she realized that kissing him this way had become one of her biggest fantasies. Slow, unhurried kisses that had nothing to do with grief or loss. A new beginning and an invitation to explore this attraction between them. Becca was grateful to learn it wasn't one-sided.

"Becca," Rick murmured against her mouth, as if claiming her. He cupped the back of her neck and the kiss became urgent. The restraint was gone, as if he realized how much she wanted him.

Becca held his face with her hands. "You don't know how long I've wanted this. I was afraid, though."

He rested his forehead against hers. "You don't ever have to be afraid with me."

"I was afraid of myself. Because I wanted this so badly."

His smile contained heat and more than a little wonder. Combined with the slow, sexy light in his eyes, it was an irresistible sight.

She raised her chin and nibbled on the corner of his mouth. Flicking his bottom lip with her tongue, she was gratified when he groaned, capturing her mouth with his.

They were so good together. Maybe it was because she was free to be herself with this man who knew her secrets, yet totally accepted her. She shifted her body in an attempt to get even closer, which was nearly impossible in the front seat of the car.

Twisting, she was able to angle herself half on top of Rick. He pulled her the rest of the way into his lap, where she straddled him, wishing she'd worn a skirt instead of pants.

Rick kissed her neck, her throat, his eyes closed, his expression tender.

How could this man care for her so deeply even after the mistakes she'd made? Becca's eyes burned with the realization that he'd been there for her every time she'd asked and many times when she hadn't, expecting nothing in return.

"I want you to know how much I care about you," she whispered.

He drew back, caressing her shoulder as he spoke. "Hey, Bec, I've always known you were a good friend. And I knew we were good together that one night. But now, I think we'd be unbelievable because our friendship has grown into something even stronger."

Lowering her eyes, Becca was almost frightened by the intensity in his. Frightened, because it perfectly reflected the way she felt about him.

He grasped her chin. "Are you okay?"

This was the man she'd known for years, a man she could trust with her life. Why was she hesitating? Especially since she'd learned all too well that life could be cut short at any time.

Raising her eyes, she said, "I'm better than okay, Rick. Because I'm with you."

His smile was sweet, yet tinged with promise.

He grasped her hips and pulled her snugly against him.

This was where Becca wanted to be more than anywhere else. She wanted to feel him inside her. Now.

He ran his hands under her blouse, cupping her breasts in his palm. His breathing was harsh in her ear, making her want him all the more.

This was crazy.

This was right.

His fingers grazed her sides, caressed her stomach. She arched her back as he trailed his tongue down the vee of her blouse.

She moved against him, gratified to feel that he was as aroused as she.

"Bec, I want you so bad." His voice was hoarse.

She pressed her finger against his lips. "Just love me." The words seemed to echo from the past, reminding her of the last time she'd been this close with him. Reminding her how right it had seemed even in the midst of chaos.

He took her finger in his mouth, sucking on the tip in a way that drove her crazy. She never, ever would have thought something so relatively benign could be so erotic.

She rocked her hips, daring him. The rhythm and friction were sweet, addictive torture.

But apparently Rick didn't agree. Grasping her shoulders, he said, "No. Not like this. Look around us."

He gestured out the window, where they were in plain sight of anyone exiting the building.

"What did we almost do?"

His chuckle was hollow. "We almost put on a pretty good show. And you know what, it would have been absolutely worth it. But you, lady, have a reputation to protect."

His slow grin warmed her heart. His concern for her reputation sealed the deal. Becca fell a little in love with Rick.

She rested her head on his chest as her breathing slowed. His heart gradually quit pounding so rapidly beneath her ear.

"You're always so good to me." Wonder tinged her voice.

"I intend to show you exactly how good I can be, making love to you in a real bed with all the time in the world. But right now, I need some space. If you ever want to make that meeting, that is."

Becca blushed to the roots of her hair when she realized she was still straddling him. And they were going to be late for their appointment anyway, because it would be more than a few minutes before Rick was meeting ready.

And for some reason, that made her smile. Or maybe it was simply the anticipation of making love with him as he'd described, with all the time in the world to explore each other and this new, deepening relationship.

CHAPTER SIXTEEN

RICK WAS ABLE to listen as the landscaping co-ordinator and Becca discussed their visions for the park. He could even add a cogent comment every once in a while.

But his mind kept coming back to the same thorny problem.

He wanted Becca.

And not just in the hot, sweaty, let's-have-a-quickie-in-the-car kind of way. He wanted a relationship with her. Out in the open, so everyone could see. He wanted to claim her as his own, refuting Gabe's previous hold on her heart.

And that was a major problem for a couple of reasons. The first was that he felt he'd failed in the friendship department by wanting to supplant his best friend. And the second was that any man who got involved with Becca at this point would raise the whispers to a dull roar. Whispers about himself Rick could handle. But

whispers about Becca could make the coming
months, even years, very difficult indeed.

Those problems were the last thing on his
mind though, when he noted her flushed cheeks
and the sparkle in her eyes and knew he'd put
them there. Then he'd recall in vivid detail how
utterly sexy it had been to have her rocking
against him in the front seat of his car. He could
have removed the interfering clothing and been
inside her in a few exquisite seconds.

"…don't you agree, Rick?"

"I'm sorry, I was thinking of something else.
What was the question?"

"We want very hardy plants, user-friendly,"
Becca said. "So if a football goes crashing into
a shrub, it won't need to be replaced."

"I agree."

"That eliminates a few of our choices." The
coordinator drew a line through several plants
on the list. "The rest of these should work aes-
thetically and still have the ability to thrive
under sometimes adverse conditions." He
handed the list to Becca.

"Wonderful." Becca beamed. "Now the fun
part begins. You'll come with me to the nursery,
won't you, Rick?"

And risk a repeat parking-lot session? It was
not a good idea for him to be alone in enclosed

spaces with her. But "Hell, yes" was on the tip of his tongue.

He managed a restrained, "Sure, if that's what you want."

"My week is pretty booked. Maybe Saturday after you play racquetball? We could get someone to cover at the agency."

"Okay."

The coordinator handed them a packet of papers. "Here's a list of the nurseries I've worked with that are willing to give us a good discount for buying in bulk. If you tell them what it's for, they might discount even deeper."

"Thank you." Becca stood and shook the man's hand.

Rick followed suit, wondering if he should have his head examined. But he had to admit, he was looking forward to spending time with Becca on Saturday. And that scared him. Because all he could think about was getting her alone in a secluded corner of the nursery. Definitely not the kind of thoughts he should be having about a pregnant widow.

ON SATURDAY MORNING, Becca selected a rolling flat cart and so did Rick.

"This was the first place on the list and it turns out they're giving us the best price, too. I stopped by on my way home from work Thursday night and liked what I saw."

"It's…nice." But Rick's focus was square on her.

She tried not to blush. But darn it, it was hard when he looked at her that way. "I had a dream last night."

"Oh, yeah?"

"It was about Gabe. He wasn't really dead. I was so happy…"

Rick glanced away. "You were always happy with Gabe. Sure, you guys had your fights. Every couple does."

"You didn't let me finish. At first, I was so happy. But then, I got upset."

"How come?"

"Because we were in the park. The landscaping was all done and beautiful, just like in the drawings the coordinator showed us."

He stopped to examine a shrub. "How'd it look?"

"Beautiful, but that's not the point. Gabe came through with a chain saw and was destroying everything we'd worked so hard to achieve."

"Interesting."

"So what does it mean?"

He raised an eyebrow. "You're asking me? Interpreting dreams really isn't my thing."

"You could give it a shot."

"Okay. Gabe 'was destroying everything we'd worked so hard to achieve.' Maybe you're a little angry with Gabe because his death almost destroyed everything you two worked together to achieve."

"Sounds feasible. But then again, dreams aren't always logical."

"What are you asking me for, then?"

"Just making conversation." Or maybe trying to provoke a reaction? See if he really cared?

Becca didn't dare tell Rick he'd figured prominently in the ending of the dream. He'd grasped her by the hand and they'd fled, with Gabe close behind, chasing them with the chain saw.

She understood the significance all too well. Her love for Gabe could destroy the new, tentative bond forming with Rick.

Or, maybe, she was simply worried about Gabe.

"Do you ever think about what heaven's like?" she asked.

"Boy, this conversation is really touching on the metaphysical."

"Maybe. I can't help but wonder if Gabe can see what I'm doing. If he approves of the way I've handled things since he's been gone. If he hates me for…well…making love with you."

Becca stopped on the pretext of examining a plant. But mostly, she wanted to avoid looking at Rick. Afraid she would see condemnation in his eyes.

Rick moved closer. "Becca, I don't know what to tell you. This isn't anything I anticipated, either. Problem is, I figured that night was an aberration. But after what happened the other day in the car, or almost happened, there's more to it than just raging hormones, even though yours would be justified."

She stepped closer and made sure her voice was low. "It's not just sex that I wanted, Rick. It's the closeness, the sharing, the feeling of safety." She touched his arm. "I have that with you."

Becca felt vulnerable and exposed, standing here in the nursery, admitting she wanted more.

"Is it enough, though?" He brushed her bangs from her forehead. "I'd like to explore what might be between us and see where it goes. But I have to admit, Gabe's a tough act to follow."

"You and Gabe are totally different and my feelings for you are different."

He stiffened. "He's dead and I'm alive."

"That's not what I meant. Comparisons are pretty much going to doom anything we may want to build. I'm more concerned about the possibility that getting involved might ruin our friendship."

"How about if we start out slow. Begin with the basics, like dating and having a good time, without going from zero to sixty in ten seconds. Our friendship should remain intact that way."

Becca smiled. "It's worth a try. We've been going about this kind of backward, haven't we? I'm not usually as…aggressive as I've been with you. It's kind of embarrassing."

He cupped her face with his hand. "Hey, I like that you find me irresistible."

"Don't let your ego get too big. It could simply be the work of all the hormones raging through my system."

"Or it could be that we have some powerful chemistry."

"I've thought of that, but…"

"But what?"

"Wouldn't there have been a hint of it before Gabe died? I always thought you were a great guy, but never had any sort of physical reaction to you until the night of Gabe's wake."

"Unless you always subliminally thought I was irresistible." He grinned, seemingly pleased with the idea.

"That's what keeps me awake at night.

Wondering if I haven't been faithful to Gabe in my heart."

"Hey, I was just kidding. Believe me, you never, ever gave off any vibes that you were anything but one hundred percent devoted to Gabe."

"Thank you. You've set my mind at ease. At least a little."

"Good." He leaned close and kissed her, all too fleetingly. "Because I intend to start pursuing you, all open and aboveboard."

"Better hurry. At the rate I'm, um, blossoming, I'll be down to a slow waddle in no time."

"All the easier to catch."

"I guess there's that."

She rested her head on his shoulder, glad that they'd arrived at a reasonable solution.

RICK WAS NERVOUS Sunday evening as he knocked on the Smith door.

And he was somewhat tongue-tied when Irene answered.

"Rick, how nice to see you. You're here for Becca?" Her words were cordial, but he thought he detected a hint of reserve.

"Yes."

"Come in. I think she's just about ready."

He followed her into the family room, disap-

pointed to see Jim seated in the easy chair.
Waiting.

"Hi, Jim."

"Hello, Rick."

At Irene's behest, he sat on the couch.

"I'll go tell Becca you're here," she said.

When she left, the silence lengthened.

Finally, Rick could stand it no more. "Did
you catch the ball game yesterday?"

"Nope. I was working in the shop."

"Oh."

Rick's foot started tapping of its own
volition. He felt as if he were a teen facing his
girlfriend's father for the first time.

"How's your, um, project going? The
memorial plaque?"

"Fine."

Man, he'd never had this hard a time talking
to Gabe's father.

Gabe's father.

Maybe it was his guilty conscience making
communication so difficult.

Rick glanced around the room, noting the
family portrait, with Gabe and Becca front
and center.

He quickly looked away.

"So, is this a date?" Jim asked.

"Yes."

"I probably don't need to remind you that Becca is vulnerable right now."

"No, sir, you don't. But I appreciate your concern."

"Do you? Do you have any idea that I want to protect Becca as if she were my own daughter? I like you, Rick. But it's too soon."

"Believe me, I've worried that it might be too soon. But I want to treat Becca with honesty and respect. And having my feelings out in the open seemed the best way to do it."

Jim raised an eyebrow. "By exposing her to needless gossip?"

"I can't control what people choose to think or say."

"But you can let things die down instead of fanning the flames. If you respect Becca as much as you say, you'll wait until after the baby is born."

Rick shook his head. "I wish it was that simple, Jim. If I could walk away from her, I would."

"So that's how it is?"

"I'm afraid so."

"Then be very sure you're good to her. I'd hate to see her heart broken right when she seems to be recovering from the shock of Gabe's death."

"I will, sir. I will."

Becca entered the room, wearing white capri pants and a turquoise top. Her hair gleamed golden beneath the overhead light. Her skin glowed. And her smile was only for him.

Rick stood, unable to utter a word. He didn't know how he'd come to be blessed by such a miracle. Becca seemed to have eyes only for him.

"You look beautiful. Let's go."

He could feel Jim's glare boring into his back as he escorted Becca from the house.

They went to his favorite little Chinese restaurant, since he recalled Becca saying she craved Chinese.

She inhaled deeply when they entered the restaurant, closing her eyes in ecstasy. "You remembered. I thought I would die if I didn't get orange chicken soon."

He cupped her elbow as they were led to their seats. "We wouldn't want that. I remember just how overpowering those cravings seem. I made more than one midnight run for fish and chips."

Becca seemed to ponder the combination. "Sounds good, but, no, this child demands orange chicken. She must've had her fill of cheeseburgers."

Their conversation turned toward the business and then her children.

"How's Aaron doing now that he's back at school?" Rick asked.

Becca crossed her fingers. "So far, so good. No more fights. He never would tell me what incited the fight."

"With boys that age, it could be almost anything."

"I'll take boys over girls any day. Maya has a new boyfriend. The other one only lasted a week."

"That might be a good thing. Not as much chance to get serious."

"Yes. But Gabe and I were serious at her age."

"You two were the exception. You married young but must have had a heck of a strong foundation."

"Yes, we did. Amazing that we were able to find that so young."

"You were the lucky ones. My brother went through a messy divorce a couple years back. I was fortunate Valerie's and mine was fairly amicable. And Kayla was grown."

Becca reached across the table and grasped his hand. "You two handled it well, when it could have been so easy to lash out."

"Valerie and I were still basically friends,

even though the love died a long time ago. We just didn't realize it until it was too late."

The waitress took their orders and they chatted about the new marketing program Rick wanted to implement for the agency.

Then a woman made a beeline for their table.

"Kim, good to see you."

Rick thought Becca's smile was a bit forced.

"Becca, you're looking wonderful. Pregnancy obviously suits you." She turned to Rick. "And you're Rick, right?"

"Yes. We met the other day outside the barbecue place."

"That's right." Kim glanced down at their clasped hands. Her smile widened. "Are you two, um...?"

"Dating," he supplied for her. "Yes, we are. Thanks for stopping by to say hello."

She tilted her head. "I better be going. See you next week, Becca. I'll look forward to hearing *all* about your date."

When she was gone, Rick raised an eyebrow. "Do you normally confide in your clients?"

"Hardly. Well, I shared a bit about how hard it was when Gabe died. But I don't kiss and tell."

"Good. That means we'll just have to give her something to talk about now."

He leaned across the table and kissed her lingeringly. His eyes held all sorts of promises.

And she had to wonder why he was so intent on going public with what was a very new and fragile relationship.

CHAPTER SEVENTEEN

THE DAY OF the company picnic arrived with clear blue skies and perfect weather.

Becca waited out front for Rick to give her a ride. Her breath caught in her throat when he got out of the SUV and walked over to her. He looked irresistible in blue jeans and a Reliable Car Rental T-shirt.

"Morning, beautiful." He kissed her on the lips, but it wasn't the passionate kiss of her dreams.

"Morning."

"What? You look disappointed."

"I am disappointed. I'd kind of hoped for more of a kiss than that. Especially since everyone in the free world knows we're dating."

He laughed, a low, gorgeous sound that sent tingles of awareness through her. Heck, his mere presence sent tingles through her.

Rick stepped closer, drawing her to him. He tipped her chin with his finger and kissed her deeply.

She closed her eyes and reveled in the feel of his lips on hers.

"Mmm."

He ended the kiss all too soon, waving to her neighbor. "No reason to give Mrs. Roberts a heart attack."

"No, she's a sweet old lady, but her timing is awful. Did you bring the coolers?"

"Yep. In the car."

"David is going to bring ours along with the soda, water and ice. The plants should be delivered any time now, so we better get going."

They arrived early so they could supervise the setup.

Becca felt energized by all the activity. This was what she loved to do—organize people, places and things to come together in a joyous event. It was like planning a family birthday party, only bigger and better.

She directed the delivery crew to set up the bouncy castle where it would be shaded in the afternoon. Experience from school events had taught her the castle could turn into an oven by afternoon.

The advance crew for the caterers had also arrived and she gave them last-minute instructions.

"Very festive," Rick's voice came from

close behind her, sending a shiver down her spine.

She turned, smiling up at him. "Exactly. Today is a happy day. A tribute to Gabe, to Reliable Car Rental and to the family we have there."

"You're amazing." He gestured to encompass the new playground equipment and the hordes of plants just waiting to be put in the ground.

Soon, families started to arrive and Becca greeted each one, handing them a shiny new trowel with Reliable Car Rental lettered on the handle. She'd bought the trowels in bulk and had paid David and Maya to apply the labels.

"Want me to spread out our picnic blanket?" Rick asked.

"You brought one, I hope. I didn't even think about it."

"Yep, sure did. Along with plenty of lawn chairs, in case there weren't enough tables."

"Thanks. I've been so distracted…"

"Hey, we're a team. You can't be expected to remember everything."

"I think I should be able to."

Rick stepped closer and kissed her briefly on the lips. "Then we'll have to change that, won't we?"

"Mmm." Becca would have agreed to almost

anything he asked. Their dinner date had been wonderful. Nothing like the few first dates she remembered from high school before she had dated Gabe. She was totally relaxed with Rick. He made it easy.

She watched him as he carried the folding chairs from the back of the car, his arms muscular, his smile wide. What a terrific guy.

Becca was drawn from her reverie by the sight of her children walking toward her, working together to carry the coolers and supplies. Seeing them gave her a warm, every-thing's-going-to-be-okay feeling.

After that, the picnic seemed to progress at warp speed. Parents chatted and laughing children took advantage of the new play-ground equipment.

"Great idea to have the picnic here, Becca," commented Joan, one of their rental agents. "It wouldn't have been the same at the water park… You know…"

Becca touched her arm. "Without Gabe. I know. I felt the same way. Did your kids see the face painting? And I think the castle is about ready to open."

Joan grinned. "Yes, bouncing before eating. Another good idea. I'll herd my kids in that di-rection. They're over there with my husband."

Becca waved at Joan's husband. "Go. Have fun."

"I could help—"

"Absolutely not. Everything's under control."

She watched Joan join her family and felt a pang of pure envy. Her life had been that way once. Now, that time seemed almost golden, a fantasy that would never happen again. But, maybe, she'd been given a second chance with Rick.

Yet there were still days she missed Gabe like crazy, and she wondered if it would always be like this.

"Why the frown?" Rick asked, handing her a bottle of water.

"Just thinking."

"Uh-oh."

"I can't help but think of Gabe today."

"That's what you intended, right? This was supposed to be a tribute."

"I know. I guess I didn't expect it to affect me this much. In some ways, my emotions are every bit as raw as the day he died. And here I've got a great guy like you and I wish I could be…normal again."

"Becca, you are normal. I don't expect you to forget Gabe. I'd worry if you didn't miss him."

"I was afraid you might think it was a bad reflection on my feelings for you."

RICK CONSIDERED Becca's point. "I'm a guy," he said. "Sure, there are times when I feel I'm competing with Gabe's memory. But I'll handle it. Why don't we just enjoy the great weather and the opportunity to honor a man who meant a lot to both of us."

Becca's smile eased the shadows in her eyes. "Absolutely."

He couldn't help but feel relieved. Because if she'd questioned him closely, he might have admitted wondering if he would always come in second best in her heart. And felt disloyal to both of his friends for feeling that way.

"Let's go get something to eat." He glanced at his watch. "Your schedule says you won't make the presentation for another half hour."

"I'm not sure I can eat. I'm too excited."

"None of that. Of course you have to eat."

"You're a stubborn man."

"I just want to make sure you take care of yourself."

"Okay. A quick bite, then more mingling."

They went by the catering tables and selected from the grilled hot dogs and hamburgers. Salads and side dishes followed, along with soda.

"How about we sit over there?" Becca motioned toward a large picnic table, where the body-shop foreman and his wife sat.

Soon, they were joined by Maya and Aaron. David was hanging out with coworkers his own age.

"Mom, Maya said I'm too big to go in the castle," Aaron complained.

Maya gave him a withering look. "You'll crush all the little-bitty kids."

"As long as you're careful of the smaller children, you can jump in the castle if you'd like. And Maya, you might be able to help out at the face-painting booth if you're bored. You have the artistic abilities for it."

Rick thought he saw a spark of interest in the girl's eyes. But she feigned disinterest, saying, "I'd rather be at home."

"Well, you're not at home, so maybe you could make an effort to enjoy yourself and be pleasant to those around you."

Maya rolled her eyes, but wisely didn't say anything.

When the presentation hour grew near, Becca stood, gathering trash. "I'll go round up the Parks and Recreation official, if you want to meet me by the plaque."

Rick gathered folks as he made his way

around the park. When he reached the make-shift podium and Becca hadn't arrived yet, he checked the portable amplifier and micro-phone.

"If you all want to gather round, Becca has an announcement to make."

The stragglers made their way over.

Becca approached with the city parks official in tow.

"Do you have scissors?" Rick asked.

She nodded, stepping up to the microphone. "Thank you all for coming today. As you know, the annual company picnic was Gabe's idea because he knew how hard you all worked and how much that contributed to our success."

Applause and whistles interrupted her. The warmth and love was almost palpable.

Becca's smile wobbled just a touch as she waited for relative quiet to descend.

"He always said that Reliable Car Rental was a family company in more ways than one. He looked forward to going to work every day and I want you to know that you meant so much to him."

Some of the women sniffled. A few of the guys cleared their throats. Rick himself had a hard time not tearing up.

"I just couldn't face a picnic at the water park

without him being there, and a few of you echoed the sentiment." Becca's voice wavered slightly, but was strong and clear when she continued. "So I thought we'd do something a little different this year. Adopting the park in memory of Gabe seems like a fitting tribute, so families in the neighborhood can enjoy picnics and camaraderie like we've enjoyed today. Their children will love the playground equipment and I'm hoping it will draw the community more tightly together."

She beckoned David forward and he began distributing the plants and planting instructions while she explained her vision.

"I'd like to introduce Marvin Jones from the City Parks and Recreation Department. He'll have some instructions for us."

The employees and their families applauded.

Rick smiled reassuringly at Becca as she headed his direction. "You did great."

"I hope so. This is really important to me."

Marvin Jones completed his short speech. "With that, we'll cut the ceremonial ribbon and let you begin. Mrs. Smith, will you join me?"

Becca removed a pair of scissors from her back pocket and grasped Rick by the hand. "Come on. You deserve to be up there, too."

Rick wasn't so sure but he followed her

anyway. He was acutely aware that he was having some decidedly competitive thoughts about a dead man, and he wasn't proud of it.

He stood back a bit when they reached the plaque, which was covered by a sheet and tied with a large, red bow.

There was a lump in his throat as he watched Becca cut the ceremonial ribbon. She lifted the sheet to display an intricate, hand-carved wooden plaque supported by four wrought-iron legs.

It read:

In Memoriam
Gabriel Smith
Loving husband, father and son. A dedicated businessman who believed in honesty, integrity and compassion.

Rick figured no one would ever memorialize him that way; he'd never felt more lacking since his best friend's death. He wanted Gabe's widow with a burning desire that had nothing to do with integrity or compassion.

CHAPTER EIGHTEEN

BECCA TENDERLY smoothed the soil at the base of the spindly sycamore tree. She could easily visualize it growing tall and strong, offering shade in the summer.

Her children stood back, silent, as if they were afraid to speak.

"What d'you guys think?" She shielded her eyes from the sunlight.

"It's awfully little," said Aaron. "Won't it need something big and strong to protect it?"

Becca got up and went over to him. "Its strength comes from being so small and flexible—it will bend, where others might break."

Aaron eyed her doubtfully.

She grasped his hand and squeezed. "It's true. And see those bigger trees over there." She pointed toward three trees growing close together. "They'll protect it from the worst of the elements."

Maya came over and grasped his other hand.

"Just like Mom, me and David are there to protect you."

Becca's eyes burned at her daughter's perceptiveness. "Exactly."

"Can we say a prayer for the tree?" Aaron asked.

"Sure." Becca's voice was husky. She hadn't had any especially fond feelings for God since he'd allowed Gabe to die. But for her son, she'd try to forgive. She extended her other hand toward David. "Come join us?"

His mouth twisted.

Becca held her breath.

Finally, he shrugged. "I guess."

He grasped her hand and pulled her toward the other side of the tree, where he linked hands with Maya. They formed a circle around the spindly little tree.

Laughter floated on the warm breeze, but it seemed to Becca as if she and her children were suspended in their own corner of the world.

Becca searched her mind for an appropriate prayer, but came up blank. "Um…"

"God," Aaron's voice rose, sure and true. "Please bless this little tree. Make sure its tree family keeps away the wind and the snow so it can grow big and strong. And please bless my daddy in heaven. Tell him we miss him. I promise not to fight anymore, so he can be proud of me. Amen."

Becca bowed her head, blinking back tears. "Amen," she murmured.

Gabe, I loved you with my whole heart and you will always be with me. I hope you understand that I need to make a new life for myself and our children. I think that's what you would want for me, too.

David cleared his throat.

Becca raised her face. All three children looked at her expectantly.

"Very nice, Aaron."

"Dad heard me?"

"I'm sure of it." She squeezed his hand. "Just as I'm sure your dad wants all of us to hold him close in our hearts and do our best to be happy. We'll come see this tree over the years and marvel at how it's grown. And we'll marvel at how *we've* grown."

"Aw, Mom, you're an adult. You can't grow no more."

"*Any*more," she corrected. Glancing down at her middle, she grinned. "And you'll be surprised at how much I'll grow in the next three months."

David released her hand. "Um, I need to go talk to somebody."

"Me, too." Maya broke away from their circle along with David.

"I'm gonna go play in the castle. I'll be careful not to crush the little kids," Aaron promised.

Becca sighed. The touching moment of family solidarity was over.

"Go. Have fun."

She watched him scamper off, amazed that he could seem so mature one minute and then a child the next.

"They're going to be okay." Rick came up beside her and slid an arm around her waist.

She rested her head briefly on his shoulder. "I think you're right."

RICK CARRIED A COOLER to Becca's garage. "Where do you want this?"

Becca turned on the light. "Over there, along that wall."

"I'll help you with the other stuff."

"That's what teenagers are for. Slave labor, or so they believe."

Chuckling, he grasped her arms and pulled her close. "It was some day, huh?"

"Yes. The best. But…exhausting."

"Are you okay?"

"Just tired. A lot of emotion today."

"I can imagine. I heard you guys say a prayer by Gabe's tree."

"I didn't realize you were that close."

Her admission wounded him, but only because his emotions were so close to the surface. He'd watched Becca and her children form a circle, knowing there was no place for him, despite the fact the kids seemed to tacitly accept his affection for their mother. He wondered what it would take for Becca to consider him part of the family.

"I was standing off to the side beyond your line of vision." Where she could have seen him if she'd simply turned her head.

"You should have joined us," Becca said, as if sensing his thoughts.

"It was a private, family time."

"You're almost family."

Almost. But not quite. The knowledge frustrated him. Because he felt that, even in death, Gabe held his family in a grip Rick would not, *could* not break. He wondered what kind of friend he'd been to even consider it.

"I better go." He drew away from her, but she grasped his arm.

"Rick?"

"What?"

"Are you okay? Are *we* okay?"

"Sure." But he couldn't quite meet her gaze

in the shadowed garage. There were too many ghosts here. "I'll call you."

"Thanks for all your help today."

"No problem."

He kissed her on the cheek and left without a backward glance. Because it hurt too much to see what might have been.

BECCA PUT ON her pajamas, which consisted of an old pair of Gabe's boxers and one of his T-shirts.

There was a knock at her bedroom door.

"Come in."

Irene entered. "How did the picnic go?"

"Perfect. I wish you and Jim had come with us."

"I wish we could have, too. But Marge and George are our oldest friends and we were attendants in their wedding. They would have been hurt if we'd begged off for their fiftieth anniversary party."

"I understand."

"Aaron said you planted a tree for Gabe and said a prayer over it."

"Yes. I'm afraid I'm not very good in the prayer department these days, so Aaron took over. He did a great job."

"He told me." Irene sat on the bed, patting the spot beside her.

Becca sat down.

Irene grasped her hand. "Things have been so busy lately, we haven't had much chance to talk. How are you doing?"

"Fine. Today was…emotional. But healing, in a way."

"Good. I only want the best for you, Becca."

"I know. How are you doing with all this?"

"I have good days and bad days. The good outnumber the bad most times."

"There was a time right after Gabe died when I was afraid there would *never* be any more good days."

"It's a choice. We choose to go on. And that's the way Gabe would have wanted it."

Becca shifted, wondering if there was a hidden meaning in Irene's words.

"That's what I told the children today."

"And how are things going with Rick?"

"Fine." She hesitated to discuss her budding romance. It seemed unkind.

"Jim is wary of Rick. He thinks it's too soon after Gabe's death and he's afraid Rick is taking advantage of your vulnerability."

"He's known Rick for years. I can't believe Jim would doubt his intentions. As a matter of fact, Rick didn't want to get involved, either. It's something we never anticipated." She glanced sideways at Irene. "And what do you think?"

"I love you like a daughter and want you to be happy."

"But?"

"But as Gabe's mother, I guess I'm a bit uneasy at the timing."

Becca willed herself not to flush. "I've done nothing wrong."

"I didn't say you had. I'm sad to see my son replaced so soon, but logically I understand it was inevitable. And I know it's my problem to work through."

Dropping Irene's hand, Becca got off the bed and stepped away from her mother-in-law. Her voice was firm when she said, "I could never, *ever* replace Gabe. This isn't like losing an old dog, then going out and getting a puppy to forget your sadness."

"What is it you feel, Becca? Do you know?" Irene's voice was gentle.

Love?

"I'm not sure. All I know is that I enjoy being with Rick. He makes me feel safe and cherished at a time when I desperately need that. I feel almost…whole again when I'm with him."

"And what does he get out of it?"

Had anyone else asked the question, Becca would have been offended. But coming from Irene, it made her stop and think.

"I honestly don't know."

"Then maybe that's something you should find out." Irene rose and left the room without waiting for an answer.

Leaving Becca with too many questions swirling in her mind.

RICK CAME IN the office after shuttling cars through the on-site car wash. He was hot, sweaty and irritable.

But his irritation vanished when he went by Becca's office.

He leaned in her doorway and said hello.

She glanced up and smiled the kind of smile that made his world tilt. The kind that told him he was the greatest guy ever.

"Hi, yourself," she said. "I went looking for you a few minutes ago."

Suppressing a surge of satisfaction, he went inside her office. Things between them had been awkward since the company picnic and he'd half suspected she'd been avoiding him.

"What's up?" he asked, glad he sounded

suitably casual. As if he hadn't missed their closeness.

"We're hosting end-of-school formal festivities Saturday afternoon and I wondered if you'd like to come over. A light, late lunch for the girls while they get ready for the dance. Apparently, all Maya's friends are coming over to primp and dress."

"Yes, I fondly remember those days."

"You're lying, aren't you?"

"Absolutely. It's torture for a father. All those giggly, squealing and sometimes tearful women-in-training. Add the usual paternal angst over potential sexcapades, and you've got an afternoon of intense torture."

Becca's eyes sparkled with amusement. "But if it's my daughter, it shouldn't be as torturous, should it?"

"No. Still not at the top of my list of things to do, but for you, anything." It was so close to the truth, his ears grew hot.

"The reason I asked was because I'll be waiting up till all hours and I thought you might be willing to keep me company."

"Absolutely." Nothing like playing hard to get. He was a goner, even knowing he might always run a far second to Gabe.

"Good."

"Anything you want me to bring?"

"Nope. I've got it under control."

CHAPTER NINETEEN

WHEN RICK ARRIVED at Becca's house, he walked inside the open front door.

Becca came in from the kitchen. "You made it."

"Yeah. There are girls everywhere."

"It sure seems like it."

"Too bad David had to work today." Rick grinned. "I imagine he'd find the scenery fascinating."

"Yes, he was quite disappointed when he saw the schedule, though I can't say having a houseful of girls was on my mind when I made it."

"Need any help?"

"Yes, I've got pop in coolers in the kitchen, if you'd ice it down."

"Sure thing." Seeing Becca in a blue-green, scoop-neck blouse made him pretty sure he should ice down his libido at the same time.

"You look beautiful." He kissed her on the lips, wishing he could kiss her more passionately without raising twenty sets of eyebrows.

"Thank you. The cleavage fairy has been very good to me this time around."

"I could lie and say I hadn't noticed. But you probably caught me staring a couple minutes ago."

Becca grinned. "I thought maybe you'd noticed." She leaned close, whispering in his ear, "At least I hoped so."

He groaned. Having her so close, her breath warm on his neck, made him want to whisk her away to a five-star hotel and make love to her all night long.

"You know what prom night means, don't you?" He raised an eyebrow.

"No, why don't you tell me." She turned and headed toward the kitchen, a saucy swing to her hips. And given her growing girth, he imagined it took some effort. Effort he definitely appreciated.

"You are an evil woman." He followed her, thinking he'd gladly follow this woman anywhere.

A few minutes later, Maya sashayed through the kitchen in her robe with several friends following closely behind. She snagged a tiny croissant sandwich from the tray and a soda from the ice chest. Frowning, she commented, "No ice."

"I'm working on it," he said, remembering what demanding taskmasters teens could be.

The girls selected food and drink, then followed Maya out of the kitchen.

"I hope you realize I'm here to save you from all the drama, if need be," he commented to Becca.

She patted him on the cheek. "I appreciate the effort. But so far, no drama."

"Just wait."

"We had the guys here to get ready for David's senior prom. They were fine."

"Are you listening to yourself, Becca? We're talking teenage *girls*. There's bound to be drama. A clothing crisis, horrible hair, a zit—it's a given. And heaven help us if one of their dates cancels at the last minute."

"I was trying to put a positive spin on it so you wouldn't run screaming from the house. Why do you think I called in the cavalry?"

"Because Gabe isn't here for one of the big nights of his daughter's life?" He stepped up behind her, resting his hands on her shoulders. "And you wanted someone here who would understand."

She turned, tears shimmering in her eyes, and walked into his open arms. "You know me too well."

Rick ignored a pang of jealousy, telling himself it was natural for Becca to still pine for her husband.

He kissed the top of her head. "Shh. It's a rough time, but you'll get through it. This was a good idea having her friends come over. With all the activity, she's not likely to focus on how much she misses her father."

"That's what I hope." Becca wiped her eyes and stepped back. "But this is just the beginning of the special occasions we'll have to get through without him. Her graduation, her wedding. She won't have anyone to walk her down the aisle."

"Hey, she has your brother, Royce. Or David. Or if worst comes to worst, she has me."

"Maya has family. She has me, too." Jim entered the kitchen and glared at Rick.

"And she's very fortunate to have such a loving grandfather," Becca said.

"So will the little one." Jim nodded toward her protruding stomach as he placed several sandwiches on a paper plate.

He gave Rick one last dismissive glare, selected a soda and left the room.

"He used to like me," Rick commented.

"You weren't competing with his son before. It's...difficult for Jim and Irene. The kids weren't too concerned when I first told them.

Maybe because you've been a part of their lives for years."

"That's great about the kids, but is Irene minding? I thought she didn't care that I was dating you."

"Most times she doesn't. But she did admit to feeling uncomfortable that I seem to be replacing Gabe so soon. I guess I can understand that."

Rick swallowed hard. He was ashamed to think that he would be very happy to replace Gabe in Becca's heart. He also knew there was little possibility of it happening. The ceremony at the company picnic had driven home that point.

"Bec, I'm under no illusion that I could ever replace Gabe. I'm hoping there's room for both of us, though."

"There's always room," she murmured.

But he had to wonder.

BECCA STRETCHED and blinked. She glanced sideways at Rick, who was sitting next to her on the couch. "Did I fall asleep?"

He grinned. "Yeah, I figured I'd take over the watch for a while."

"I didn't drool or anything, did I?"

"Only a little."

Wiping her mouth, she was relieved to find he was teasing her. "That wasn't nice."

Shrugging, he said, "I'm allowed a little fun every now and then. Besides, I have to amuse myself somehow when I'm the only person awake in the house."

"Did Jim and Irene go to bed?"

"An hour ago."

"I've been asleep that long? I'm so sorry. Usually I can stay awake. But with the baby and all, I've had a heck of a time staying up past ten o'clock."

"Don't worry. You don't need to entertain me."

When he'd gotten bored with TV, he'd had a stare down with the photo of Gabe. Gabe had finally won. What that said, Rick didn't know.

"Still, that was pretty rude of me. You're a good guy."

"Don't ever forget it. What time's Maya supposed to be home?"

"One o'clock."

"It's only eleven now. You've got plenty of time to play hostess."

Becca rested her head on his shoulder. "Thanks for being here tonight. It means a lot."

"Quit thanking me already. I'm here because I want to be."

"And why is that?" She tipped her head back to look up at him.

"Why do I want to be here?"

"Yes."

"That's easy. Because you're here. You're smart and beautiful and fun to be with. That, and my penchant for rescuing damsels in distress."

Becca didn't like Rick's characterization of her. "Since when do I need to be rescued?" She raised her hand. "No, don't answer that. I guess being suddenly widowed then finding out I'm pregnant at forty-one technically qualifies me for damselhood. But I *will* make it work."

"I never had any doubt."

She wondered how to phrase the question that had been bothering her for days.

"Irene said something the other day that got me thinking. She wanted to know what you got out of our relationship. I have to wonder the same thing."

He made a noise low in his throat.

"It's not like I'm a real catch right now," she added.

"I'm sure Irene didn't mean it that way." He tapped the tip of her nose with his finger. "And as far as I'm concerned, you are absolutely irresistible."

The sincerity in his eyes went a long way toward easing her doubts.

"I'm not being very fair to you." There, it was

out. "You should be dating someone who has more to give than I do."

"I don't see it that way."

"I'm lost and lonely and I've taken advantage of our friendship."

"It would only be taking advantage if I weren't aware of that. Believe me, I've considered the fact that I might be your rebound guy."

"No, Rick, it's nothing like that."

"Isn't it? Gabe's death broke your heart. It hit you out of the blue. You're a woman with a lot of love to give and you allowed me to reach out to you."

"I can't believe this is how you view our relationship. How you view me."

"Bec, I saw you at the picnic. I know you were the love of Gabe's life and vice versa. I can handle that."

"It breaks my heart that you want so little from me. That you're willing to settle for simply being a rebound guy."

His voice was rough when he said, "It's better than not being in your life at all."

"Besides the obvious fact that we own a business together, there is no way I'd push you away like that."

"I can think of one reason."

"What?"

He glanced at the stairway. "Look, I promised I wouldn't bring it up again. Particularly not here. Why don't we forget I said anything?"

Becca was tempted to do just that. She suspected it was something she didn't want to hear. But she also knew it was important if they were to go forward. And Becca was pretty sure she wanted to move forward with Rick.

"No. We need to talk now."

Rick held her gaze, then slowly nodded. "Is there anywhere we can be sure we won't be overheard?"

Uneasiness skittered down Becca's spine, but she ignored it. This was too important. They needed to hash this out once and for all.

"The guesthouse. Come on."

She stood, extending her hand.

RICK TWINED his fingers in Becca's, wanting to hold on too tightly. Particularly when they walked past the family photograph.

He could almost swear he felt Gabe's gaze follow them to the kitchen.

Becca grabbed a key off the hook and removed a flashlight from the drawer. "Don't want to wake Jim and Irene turning on the floodlights."

"No." Definitely not.

Becca flicked on the flashlight as they walked out the door.

He followed, silently, hyperaware of Gabe's parents sleeping in the basement. He'd had a hard enough time wrapping his head around the thought of having a relationship with Becca, without Jim and Irene clouding the waters.

Becca unlocked the door to the guesthouse and he stepped inside after her. The air was slightly stale and hung like dead weight.

Pulling the chain on a ceiling fan, she turned to him, her face illuminated by the weak moonlight coming through the window. She closed the curtains, then turned on the light over the stove in the attached kitchenette.

It wasn't very bright, but he could see her expression.

"Now, let's finish that conversation." Becca raised her chin in challenge. All it made him want to do was kiss her until she forgot the stupid discussion.

But he didn't and she didn't.

Raising an eyebrow, she asked, "So what is the one reason you think I would push you away?"

"You really want to know?"

"Yes."

"I could have made a big damn deal about

this baby and demanded that you consider the possibility that it's mine."

"I did consider it, you know that. You also know that its being yours is virtually impossible."

"Not as impossible as you want both of us to believe. Things were so…spontaneous that night. Neither of us was thinking straight. I barely got the condom on in time and… well…may not have done the best job putting it on."

"It was fine. I would have known…if there had been a failure."

"You're sure about that? Things were so heated and you were out of your mind with grief."

"If you had such strong doubts, why didn't you tell me all this before?"

"I tried, but you had your mind made up from the word go. And I allowed myself to believe you were right because I knew the challenges you would face if the baby was mine."

"There's more, isn't there?"

He hesitated. "I was afraid I'd lose you completely if I pushed."

Becca rubbed her arms as if she was cold. "Then why are you doing it now?"

"Because I want you too much. Not just friendship, not just a casual relationship, I want to take it to the next level." He stepped close to her, gently grasping her arms. "I have the feeling you want the same thing, too."

"What if that's not what I want? What if I've changed my mind?"

"I don't think you have. You tried to seduce me twice. There's something intense between us that just can't be written off."

"I can't deny that. But I won't listen to talk about the baby not being Gabe's. It *has* to be his."

"Don't you think I understand that? Don't you think I wish with all my heart we could be one hundred percent sure? If we were, I could devote myself to you and promise to raise his child as my own. But what if it *is* my child? Would you expect me to raise my child as if it were someone else's?"

Becca tried to pull away, but he wouldn't release her. "I can't think about this. It's too much." Her voice broke. Tears shimmered in her eyes.

The sheer pain he was inflicting on her sliced through him. He couldn't hold out against her pain.

"I know it's too much… I've always known. And still I want you. What does that say about me?"

"That you're kind and compassionate. That you care about me."

"Oh, yes, I care about you." More than she would probably ever know. "And for that reason, I'll believe as you believe."

He dipped his head and kissed her with all the hunger in his soul, attempting to erase the traces of Gabe standing between them.

"Rick…" Her voice was edged with need.

He could feel her pulse pounding beneath his thumb where he caressed her jaw. He could hear her quick intake of breath as his fingers trailed down her throat.

Heat rushed through him as she drifted closer, until her pregnant belly came in contact with his groin. He wrapped his arms around her and drew her tightly against him, finding primitive satisfaction in her moan of capitulation.

CHAPTER TWENTY

BECCA WAS TOUCHED that Rick would set aside his doubts for her. She surrendered to the moment, wrapping her arms around his neck and returning his kiss with a tender passion that shouldn't have surprised her.

She wanted to be with him tonight. Not with the obsessive hunger she'd felt with him before. But with a need to share herself body and soul with a man. A man she feared she was falling in love with.

It was intoxicating to be held by a man who wanted her every bit as badly as she wanted him. One who cherished her with tender caresses and murmured endearments. One who seemed willing to give his all for her. It reminded her of the early days with Gabe, though she had been so young at the time.

Becca pushed the thought away, determined to be in the moment with Rick and appreciate him without ghosts from the past interfering.

Rick broke off the kiss.

"How long do we have?" His breathing was uneven.

She glanced at her watch. "An hour and a half."

Smiling, he nibbled the corner of her mouth. "That might be enough time."

Becca's pulse raced at the promise in his tone. "I'll hold you to that. Unless, of course, Maya arrives home before curfew."

"And how many times has that happened?"

"Zero."

"So, I think we're safe." He rested his forehead against hers. "I want to make love with you in a real bed, taking our time, learning about each other."

"Me, too." She grasped his hand. "The bedroom is this way."

She opened the blinds a crack to let in slivers of moonlight to illuminate the room. Then she led him to the bed, letting go of his hand while she drew her shirt over her head. His dark gaze followed her movements as she skimmed out of her shorts.

Becca was glad she'd splurged on a new maternity bra and panty set, more pretty than utilitarian.

Rick seemed to appreciate them, too, because he smiled slowly as he viewed her from head to toe. "You are so beautiful," he murmured.

"Your turn."

He removed his shirt and jeans in no time, taking a small packet from his pocket. Then he stood before her in tight briefs that almost glowed white in the moonlight.

Stepping closer, he caressed her round belly, his fingers skimming lightly, raising goose bumps. The baby kicked in response.

"Was that—"

"Yes." She grasped his hand and placed it in prime kicking territory.

Sure enough, a few seconds later, the baby kicked again.

"Wow. I'd forgotten how totally miraculous the whole process is."

"Me, too." Becca ran her hands up his biceps and across his chest, reveling in the feel of warm flesh and hard muscle. Heat suffused her, along with a need so intense it took her breath away.

She kissed the side of his neck, pressing closer, but not nearly close enough.

"This—" he flicked open the clasp of her bra "—has to go."

The cool air made her nipples pucker in anticipation of his touch.

He caressed her breasts while he nudged her backward.

She reclined on the bed and he straddled her, holding her gaze, promising her everything.

Rubbing his thumbs across her breasts, he smiled at her indrawn breath.

It had been so long.

She arched against him as sensations flooded her.

When he leaned close and circled her nipple with his tongue, she thought she might come unglued. The ultrasensitivity of pregnancy made her whimper with need.

Rick moved to her rib cage, teasing her with kisses in a seemingly random pattern, yet dipping lower and lower. His tongue swirled where her navel was no longer quite so concave.

Reaching for him, she was surprised when he gripped her wrist.

"Not tonight. I'm more than ready. I want you to be the same way."

"I am." Her voice was raw, raspy and unfamiliar, as if she'd had a scotch and a few cigarettes.

He slid his fingers inside her panties and sucked in a breath when his thumb brushed her core.

She arched against him, hoping he got the

message. It seemed as if she'd been waiting for him forever.

His motions were slow, circular and drove her wild.

Arching up, she caught his mouth in a hungry kiss, stroking him with her tongue, murmuring encouragement.

When she didn't think she could stand a moment longer, he stopped caressing.

Becca opened her eyes and rose up on her elbows.

He pulled a condom from a packet and slid it on.

Raising an eyebrow, she joked. "I can't get any more pregnant than I already am."

He covered her with his body, framing her face with his hands. "I should have a clean bill of health, but you can never be too careful. I want to be one hundred percent sure you and the baby are safe."

Becca fell a little more in love with Rick in that moment. "You are so good to me."

"Oh, I intend to be even better than good." With a long, fluid stroke, he was inside her.

Becca wrapped her legs around him, drawing him in, aching with a need that scared her. She'd worried that it might seem all wrong. Worried that she would compare him to Gabe and find him lacking. But he was simply Rick. And they fit together perfectly.

RICK CRANKED AN EYE open and glanced at his watch. He kissed the top of Becca's head.

"We must've dozed off," she whispered. "What time is it?"

"Twelve-thirty. So much for making love with you all night. I've been waiting for you so long, I took things faster than I intended."

She smiled, caressing his chest with her fingertips. "If I remember correctly, I told you to hurry."

"Yeah, but a gentleman would have ignored you."

"I'm glad you didn't." She nipped at his chest.

He yelped playfully. "We have another half hour. What do you think? Shall we give it another try?"

She giggled a very un-Becca-like giggle.

He threw his leg over her. "Is that a yes?"

"Shh. I didn't say anything."

That's when he realized it hadn't been Becca's giggle he'd heard. There was a thump against the front wall, followed by another giggle. It came from outside.

"Stay here." He rose.

Becca grabbed his hand. "Rick, no."

"I'm going to check it out," he whispered.

"Don't you think you ought to put on some clothes first? Especially since we want to keep this part of our relationship…private?"

"Um, you have a point."

He drew on his pants and grabbed his shirt.

They heard a key turning in the lock.

"Damn." Becca scrambled for her clothes, no longer smiling. As a matter of fact, he could have sworn he saw fear flash in her eyes.

After their recent conversations, he hoped like hell it wasn't Jim or Irene at the door.

Rick buttoned his shirt, watching Becca climb into her shorts.

She ran her hand over the sheets but came up empty. Shrugging, she pulled her top on over her head, going braless beneath.

Rick sighed with regret as she covered those gorgeous breasts.

He heard the front door click shut and someone in the kitchenette.

Glassware clinked. Then whispered conversation.

Rick turned, ready to confront the intruders, though he had a pretty good idea who it was. Prom night. An empty guesthouse. The equation wasn't difficult.

Becca grabbed his arm. "Shoes," she mouthed, glancing down at his bare feet.

He nodded and retrieved his shoes. Where his socks were was anybody's guess. Probably cavorting with Becca's missing bra. Oh, and what a wonderful bra it had been. His groin tightened as he recalled how gorgeous she'd been in the lacy wisps of lingerie…

Becca nudged him and frowned in warning.

Oh, yes, serious business at hand.

He pulled on his shoes and led the way to the front room.

His suspicions were confirmed by the couple making out on the sofa. Two wine coolers sat on the counter, condensation beading the bottles.

More whispered endearments, laced with giggles.

Becca moved around him and opened her mouth.

Rick placed a finger over her lips to silence her. Grasping her hand, he pulled her into the bedroom. "Think this through," he murmured close to her ear. "They might not even come into the bedroom."

Her eyes widened. She pressed her mouth to his ear. "What if my daughter loses her virginity on the couch?"

"There is that."

Damn.

Becca hesitated for a nanosecond.

Then she straightened her shoulders, turned and stalked back into the front room, flipping on the overhead light as she went.

Rick had never been as impressed with her bravery as he was now. Because they were truly and totally screwed.

He followed close behind, protecting her back as she entered the lion's den.

"What is the meaning of this, Maya?"

The couple sprang apart.

Maya straightened her clothes, the boy merely blinked stupidly.

"M-mom. What are you doing here?"

"The more pressing question is what are *you* doing here, young lady?"

"We, um, just came here to talk."

"Don't insult my intelligence." Becca's retort cracked like a whip.

Rick's admiration grew.

Maya crossed her arms. "We wanted to be alone. Is that a crime?"

"Do I allow you to be at your boyfriend's house when his parents aren't home?"

"What's that got to do with it?"

Maya was pretty good with the answer-a-question-with-a-question defense, but he knew she would be no match against Becca.

Becca crossed her arms and actually tapped her toe. "Don't play stupid with me, Maya. It's offensive and makes me even angrier than I already am. Unsupervised teens sometimes indulge in impulsive sexual activity."

"Mom! That's not why we're here!"

"And what about the alcohol?"

"It's just wine coolers."

Oh, wrong answer.

Becca addressed the boy. "I think you'd better leave."

That was all the invitation the boy needed. He was out the door practically before the words left Becca's lips.

"Maya, we'll discuss this up at the house."

Maya stood. "This isn't fair." She glanced at Rick for the first time. "What's he doing here?"

She surveyed Becca's tousled hair. Then she eyed Rick from the top of his head to the tips of his sockless feet.

"You missed a button," she said to him.

He glanced down and found that Maya was right. His shirt looked as if it had been buttoned by a three-year-old.

She stalked past him to the bedroom, victory blazing in her eyes.

They were toast.

"Maya, I said wait up at the house for us."

"Mom, do you want to explain this?"

Becca turned to him.

He shrugged. "Better face the music," he whispered.

They walked into the bedroom and Rick wished the floor would open up and swallow him whole.

Maya stood by the unmade bed, twirling Becca's lace bra on her forefinger.

They were so busted.

CHAPTER TWENTY-ONE

TIME SEEMED to stand still as Becca watched her prized new maternity bra rotating on her daughter's finger. The contempt she saw on Maya's face made her want to squirm.

She opened her mouth to speak, but clamped it shut. What was there to say?

Slowly, Maya stopped twirling the bra, allowing it to hang limply on her finger, like a discarded surrender flag. She glanced at the rumpled bed and apparently spied another piece of evidence, because she pounced.

Becca swallowed hard when Maya turned and slowly opened her hand to reveal a square wrapper.

"At least you used protection, Mom. It's good you practice *something* you preach." Her lip curled.

Rick stepped forward. "You shouldn't talk to—"

"I'll handle this." Much as Becca appreciated

his gesture, she knew this was her battle. And, on second thought, they'd better hash it out here, without Maya's brother and grandparents within listening range.

"Maya, I am an adult. I'm neither promiscuous nor stupid. When I choose to enter into a sexual relationship, I do it for the right reasons. Not because it's prom night and I've had a wine cooler or two."

"That's so—"

"True. Can you honestly tell me you love this boy?"

"Can you honestly tell me you love Rick?"

Becca itched to slap her daughter. She could almost feel the satisfying sting and that appalled her. She'd never struck her children in anger. "My feelings are private, between me and Rick."

"Ditto. My relationships are none of your business."

Becca stepped closer, practically trembling in anger. "When you are an adult and no longer live in my home, then your sex life won't be my business. But until then, it's absolutely my concern and don't you ever forget it."

Maya glared back at Becca, but glanced away. Her prom-induced defiance was fading quickly. Becca hoped she was realizing this was a battle she couldn't win.

Because, fair or not, the cards were stacked in Becca's favor.

RICK WATCHED Maya stalk up the walkway.

He grasped Becca's hand to give her courage. "That was a tough scene."

Becca nodded, her mouth a tight line.

They absolutely needed to talk, but not tonight.

Maya flung open the kitchen door.

Light blazed through the opening. Rick didn't recall that many lights when he and Becca had tiptoed outside.

He stopped short when he entered the kitchen. "Jim, Irene."

"I'm sorry," Becca said. "I hope we didn't wake you."

"No, but you sure as hell worried us," Jim said, his expression thunderous. "I don't sleep well until all my girls are home safe and sound. I came up here for a drink and the place was deserted. No Becca, no Maya."

"I didn't mean to worry you. We were... checking on something in the guesthouse."

Becca was a horrible liar and Rick loved her for it. Even if it did make his life difficult at the moment.

"Yes, I can vouch for her." Maya smiled sweetly. "I have a date tomorrow with Justin. That should be okay, shouldn't it, Mom?"

Becca hesitated. He could tell she was tempted to take advantage of Maya's blackmail offer—her silence in return for a pardon.

Heck, Rick was all for it. Except it wouldn't set a good precedent. Closing his eyes for a moment, he was glad it wasn't his call.

"Rick, what do you think? Should I let her go?"

Rick opened his eyes to see mischief lurking in Becca's eyes. And resignation.

"This is a child-rearing question. Not my call."

"But I'm inviting your opinion."

He sighed. This was a no-win situation. "Then I would say do what you feel is right and we'll accept responsibility for the consequences."

"Mom," Maya protested, "don't listen to him. This is really such a minor thing in the grand scheme of things. We've all learned a lesson tonight. Let's leave it at that."

Becca tapped her chin with her forefinger. "I'm having the lock on the guesthouse rekeyed first thing in the morning. And I'm grounding you for two weeks for your lapse in judgment."

"What about *your* lapse in judgment?"

"Like I told you, I'm an adult and responsible for my own actions."

"So it's okay for you to be sleeping with some man only a few months after Dad died?" Her voice rose. "Having sex with him when your children are asleep a few yards away? When your in-laws are almost in the same house?"

Irene gasped.

Jim muttered a curse.

Becca's face reddened. She squared her shoulders and shut the kitchen door. "I would really prefer not to share my private life with everyone in the neighborhood. But since you brought it up, I'll address the issue. I certainly don't want to make Jim and Irene uncomfortable. And I will do everything possible to provide a stable home life for you children. But I will not crawl off into a corner and die of grief, no matter how much I loved your father."

Silence descended.

Rick could hear the kitchen clock tick.

There was no way he was going to enter into the fray. Unless, of course, Becca needed his protection.

Jim was livid. "I—"

Irene interrupted him. "Jim and I believe it would be best if we got an apartment in a retirement village. We'll be out of here as soon as possible."

Becca shook her head. "That wasn't what I meant. I don't want you to leave. It wouldn't be the same around here without you."

Rick ached at the thought of Becca experiencing yet another loss. He grasped her hand. "Maybe we did let things move too fast between us. Why don't we back off for a while. Go back to being friends. There's no need for anyone to move out."

"I don't want to go back to the way things were, but I don't want to lose Jim and Irene, either."

Irene rose. "Becca, it's apparent you need your privacy. We've imposed long enough. Now, if you'll excuse me, I'd like to go back to bed." She walked stiffly from the room.

Jim followed, but not before throwing a glare over his shoulder in Rick's direction.

Crap.

He'd royally messed up Becca's life when all he'd wanted to do was love her.

BECCA PUNCHED the pillow and rolled onto her other side. The baby kicked energetically.

She caressed a knobby knee or elbow. "What are we going to do, little one?"

The baby responded by kicking her hand.

Becca smiled. "You're a fighter, that's for sure. You must have gotten your courage from your father, because you sure didn't get it from me."

The baby quieted.

The night seemed silent and lonely. If only Gabe were here. If only Rick were here. Maya had been right. How could she possibly care for Rick so deeply only months after Gabe died? She must be a horrible person.

Then an awful thought occurred to her, an insistent echo of a conversation she'd had with Rick.

Even if he hadn't noticed anything out of the ordinary in her previous behavior, what if she'd *always* been attracted to Rick on some level and simply denied her attraction until Gabe died? And then the minute she was free, she'd jumped Rick's bones?

Becca squeezed her eyes shut, thinking back to the many times Rick had been a guest in their home. Trying to recall anything but platonic friendship.

The first swim party.

She'd noticed how utterly attractive he was in his swim trunks. Tanned, muscular and the epitome of male beauty. But Gabe had come up and wrapped his arms around her and she'd totally forgotten Rick.

Was she really that fickle? Out of sight, out of mind? And once Gabe was out of sight, she'd gone straight to the next guy on the list.

Who was she trying to fool? She had no right to set moral standards for anyone. And that was a very scary place for a parent to be.

RICK TRIED not to watch for Becca to arrive on Monday, but he must have been tuned in on some level, because he noticed a difference the minute she entered the building. There seemed to be an extra hum of electricity, as if the very air were charged.

Shaking his head, Rick realized he had it bad.

He watched her go through the customer waiting area toward her office. He half rose, wanting to follow. But then he sat down, determined not to crowd her. He'd caused enough trouble in her life.

He'd just managed to lose himself in profit projections, when there was a tap on the door frame.

Becca leaned in, her smile strained. "Got a minute?"

"Sure. Come on in."

She closed the door behind her.

Rick drew a deep breath, preparing himself for the total kiss-off.

"I had a doctor's appointment this morning."

"Is everything okay? Can I get you a glass of water or something?"

Becca chuckled hollowly. "I may take a rain check for that water until Thursday."

"You didn't answer my question. What's wrong? What did they find?"

"One of my tests came back as positive. False positives are fairly common, so we don't know for sure that anything's wrong, but since this is a high-risk pregnancy, the doctor wants to do another ultrasound."

Releasing his breath, Rick said, "You had me scared there for a minute."

"I was…concerned, too."

The fact that she chose her words carefully told him she must have been more than concerned. Probably downright terrified.

"They couldn't get you in any sooner for the ultrasound?"

She shook her head.

"I'm sorry you've had a scare, Bec. Was anyone with you at the doctor's office?"

"No, it was just a routine visit."

"I hate to think of you being there alone and hearing there might be potential problems."

"It was…hard. Normally I'm not a wuss about this kind of stuff. When I was pregnant before, I never expected Gabe to go to my appointments with me, like I've heard some women do. But so many things are different with this pregnancy and I have to admit I'm nervous what the ultrasound might show. I'm determined to raise this child whether it has special needs or not, but I'm just…nervous."

Hearing Becca admit to being scared touched off all sorts of protective instincts. If she were his wife, he'd be right there beside her for this sort of thing, prepared to console her—and himself—if the news was bad.

"I kind of wondered…." She shook her head. "But, it's too much to ask."

"What?"

"Would you go with me to the ultrasound appointment on Thursday?"

Rick swallowed hard. He wasn't Becca's husband, and in all likelihood wasn't the baby's father. Was he prepared to be there to see images of Gabe's child cocooned in Becca's womb?

Her eyes grew bright. She blinked rapidly. "I shouldn't have asked—it might start gossip if someone saw us together there. Normally, I would ask... Never mind. I shouldn't have asked. It was silly of me to even think you would want to. Normally, I would ask Irene, but things have been pretty strained since Saturday night. And somehow, Maya didn't seem like the right choice, either. She and I have barely spoken. I was going to ask Susan at work, but she's off to Cabo, and—"

"I don't want you exposed to gossip, but your physical well-being comes first. I'll go, but I promise to stay very low key." He couldn't stand the thought of Becca facing that kind of news alone. It would be difficult, but he would go. For Becca. Only for Becca.

"Y-you'll go?"

"Yes. What time shall I pick you up?"

"Eight-thirty?"

He rummaged on his desk for a pen, all thumbs for some reason. Finally finding one, he wrote the appointment on his desk calendar. "There. It's official. Eight-thirty on Thursday."

CHAPTER TWENTY-TWO

ON THURSDAY MORNING, Becca waited in the driveway for Rick to arrive. That way there was less chance he would run into Irene or Jim. It was cowardly on her part, but she wasn't feeling particularly brave these days. Preparing herself for the possible results of the ultrasound had been harder than she'd anticipated. Fear of the unknown was raising all sorts of doubts.

Rick's SUV pulled into the driveway, giving her a reprieve from her anxieties.

She had the passenger door open before he had a chance to shut off the engine. Waving to her neighbor, she climbed in and closed the door quickly behind her.

"I would have helped you in."

"Did I look like I needed help?" The question was downright bitchy, but she couldn't seem to help herself. "I won't need a hoist for at least a couple more weeks."

Rick grinned. "Good morning to you, too."

"You needn't be so cheery." Sighing, she said, "I'm sorry. I didn't sleep much last night."

"Me neither." He reached over and patted her hand. "But everything will be fine."

"I know I said I'm prepared to raise this baby no matter what, but you've seen how I've mishandled everything since Gabe died. How could God possibly believe I would be an adequate parent for a special-needs child? And speaking of God, what if he's punishing me? For making love with you the first time. Then there's the whole disaster in the guesthouse Saturday night."

"The whole evening wasn't a disaster. Up until Maya showed up, I thought it went pretty well."

"Leave it to a man to zero in on being good in bed when there are real problems brewing. I should have known."

"Okay, I'll stop kidding. I thought maybe I might be able to joke you out of your fears. Wrong approach."

"Obviously." Becca crossed her arms, hoping she didn't start crying. "I'm sorry, too. I seem to have two settings these days—bitchy and blubbering. I can go from one to the other in a matter of seconds."

Rick threaded his fingers through hers and squeezed. "It'll be okay, Bec. Whatever happens, I'm here for you. Never doubt that."

Becca wished she found his words reassuring. But her sense of security had come from a long-term marriage, bound together by marriage license, children and mortgage. Rick's promises, though well meaning, were light in comparison. Especially since she'd never felt so vulnerable in her life.

"Your doctor's over on Second Street, isn't she?"

"Yes."

"When my ex-wife was pregnant, we had to go to an imaging place to have her ultrasound."

"My obstetrician's practice is part of a larger OB clinic—they have their own machine. It was broken last time, so I had to go to the hospital."

"Oh."

It seemed to take forever to get there.

Becca winced when they went over a speed bump.

"You okay? You're not in labor or anything, are you?" The panic in his voice would have been comical if her sense of humor hadn't fled.

"Yes, I'm fine. I have enough water sloshing around inside to swamp a dinghy. It's a little hard on the kidneys."

"I forgot about that part."

"It's all coming back to me too clearly. I'm

having some pretty strong recollections of labor, too. I thought I was done with this after Aaron."

"We plan and God laughs. Oh, and what you were talking about earlier? You're not being punished, Becca. This baby will have ten fingers and ten toes and be absolutely beautiful, I'm sure of it."

"But what if it isn't okay?" Becca whispered, almost afraid to tempt fate by putting her worries into words.

"Then you'll have lots of help. I'll be there and the baby will have three adoring older siblings. And four adoring grandparents."

"Irene and Jim are barely speaking to me. It's as if they're cutting me out of their lives."

"They'll come around. And your dad and stepmom seemed very supportive at the funeral."

"Yes, but they have their own life in Florida."

"No more buts. Let's think positive, okay?"

She squeezed his hand. "Thank you. I don't know what I'd do without you today. I'm extremely nervous."

"Yeah, I got that impression. But I probably would be, too, if I were in your shoes."

They pulled into the lot and parked in front of the doctor's office. Rick had the engine shut off and was around to open her door before she could grasp the handle.

He extended his hand.

She glanced at it and giggled. Suddenly, his chivalry tickled her sense of the ridiculous.

"What?"

"No hoist and sling?"

"Absolutely not. I'm a gentleman."

Patting his cheek, she said, "Yes, you are." His arm felt warm and reassuringly stable beneath her palm.

Her breath caught in her throat as she gazed straight into his eyes, noticing for the first time the flecks of gold. He was one gorgeous man.

Rolling her eyes, Becca wished the mood swings would ease a bit. She'd gone straight from wanting to kill him to wanting to nest with him.

She shook her head. "We'd better get inside before I try to take advantage of you in the front seat again."

"With all that water sloshing around? No, thanks."

"Where's your sense of adventure?"

"Dealing with your moods is plenty of adventure for me." He helped her out of the car and continued to hold her arm as they approached the door. "Were you this…changeable with your other pregnancies?"

"Yep. Gabe used to call me Sybil."

"And you didn't deck him?"

"No, 'cause he kept me supplied with bacon and Ho Hos."

"That's all it took? Bacon and Ho Hos? You're a cheap date."

"Not so cheap this time around. Orange chicken has given way to shrimp and those fluffy pink snowball cupcakes. Not together, of course."

"Figures you'd have the expensive cravings on my watch. I aim to please, though."

She stopped at the door, waiting for him to open it, gazing into his gorgeous eyes. "Because I'm worth it."

He smiled, his expression slightly dazed. "You sure are."

RICK'S NERVOUSNESS faded, replaced by total awe, as he watched the screen. "I can see tiny hands. It's sucking its thumb."

"Isn't it beautiful?" Becca breathed.

"You're sure you don't want to know the sex?" the technician asked.

"Yes." Rick could have kicked himself. It wasn't his call to make and he'd jumped in as if it were.

"No," Becca said.

The technician looked confused. "Which is

it? Yes you want to know, or no you don't want to know?"

"We don't want to know." Becca's voice was firm.

Rick suppressed a pang of curiosity. He shrugged.

"Your husband doesn't seem convinced."

"He's not my, um, husband. Or the baby's father."

"Oh. I just thought, well, never mind." The technician busied herself punching in commands on the keyboard.

Rick was glad, because suddenly the room seemed way too small. And too warm. All he wanted to do was escape the overwhelming sense of loss that had accompanied Becca's statement. He wasn't her husband. He wasn't the baby's father.

He was nobody.

BECCA'S FINGERS shook as she dressed. Rick, the perfect gentleman, had gone to wait in the hall. She intended to tease him mercilessly about that after they talked to the doctor. If the news was good, that is. If it was bad, she didn't know what she would do.

After using the connected restroom, she stepped into the hall, smoothing her hair, straightening her blouse. "The doctor's office is this way."

He nodded.

"You're awfully quiet."

"It was kind of an awe-inspiring event."

"Yes, it was." She touched his arm. "Thank you for coming with me."

"No reason you should go alone."

Glancing sideways, she wondered what made him so subdued. Was he afraid of doctor's offices? Or simply concerned about what the ultrasound might reveal, even though the technician had given them the thumbs-up sign?

"I want to take you to dinner tonight. To thank you for being such a big help."

He frowned. "It was nothing, Becca. Nothing."

"Why do I get the feeling there's something you're not telling me?"

"I'm fine. Sometimes guys get moody, too."

She nudged him with her elbow. "I've always known that. You're just the first man who has ever admitted it."

But instead of smiling, he grew cooler, if that was possible. Uneasiness made her tummy rumble, which in turn prodded the baby into action.

"Just let it go," he said.

"Okay. You will let me buy you dinner

tonight, though, won't you? Provided the doctor confirms everything is okay."

He hesitated, then rolled his eyes. "You don't give up, do you?"

"No."

"Then the answer is yes. Of course I'll let you buy me dinner tonight."

Becca could almost feel the tension between them evaporate. In turn, her mood lightened. Everything was going to be okay. And that's exactly what the doctor confirmed when they met with her.

BECCA WAS PUTTING the finishing touches on her makeup when Maya knocked on her bedroom door and entered. She leaned in the doorway to the bathroom.

"Hey, Mom."

"Hi, sweetie. Did you rent some movies for you and Aaron?"

"After being grounded for almost a week, rented videos will seem like a cool night. I don't know if I can handle being responsible for the twerp that long, though. He gets annoying."

"Only when you're trying to talk on the phone. And you don't have phone privileges, so it shouldn't be a problem. It'll be good for you to spend some time with him."

"I don't know why you couldn't just ask Grandma and Grandpa to watch him."

"In case you haven't noticed, things have been a bit…strained. Since they don't approve of my social life, it would be pretty rude to ask them to babysit while I go out on a date."

Maya wrinkled her nose. "I see your point."

"Besides, you're grounded, so you're available."

"To be your slave."

"Yes, in a manner of speaking."

Becca applied her mascara, trying to keep her tone casual. "You're okay with me dating Rick?"

"I guess. I mean, at least it's someone we've known almost forever. Besides, Aaron and I talked about it, and I think he's relieved to have Rick around."

"I'm glad. No one will ever take your dad's place, but young boys need a father figure."

Maya went and sat cross-legged on the bed. "Mom?"

"What?"

"What's the big deal about a bone marrow transplant? I mean, it's just a regular operation, isn't it? They take the old stuff out and put in the new?"

"It's a little more complicated than that from

what I understand. I think they kill the old bone marrow and that leaves the person vulnerable to infection. And sometimes the body will reject the new marrow, just like it would a donated organ. Why do you ask?"

"Jennifer's brother needs one."

Becca closed her mascara and went to her daughter. She sat down and grasped Maya's hands. "I'm sorry to hear that."

Maya's lips trembled. "Is he going to die?"

"Oh, honey. I don't know anything about what he's going through. But a bone marrow transplant is usually serious. Do you know why he needs it?"

"Leukemia or something like it. Jennifer's not a match and neither are her parents because Brandon's adopted. They say family's usually the best match."

"I've heard that's true. It must be terrible for her family, wanting so badly to help."

"Jennifer's scared they won't find a donor in time." Maya started to cry. "Brandon's annoying sometimes like Aaron, but I don't want him to die."

Becca enfolded her in a hug. "Nobody does, honey. I bet Jennifer's glad to have a good friend like you to talk to. If you hear of anything we can do to help, let me know."

Her daughter nodded, resting her head on Becca's shoulder. At times like these, it seemed as if there had never been a difficult moment between them.

CHAPTER TWENTY-THREE

RICK WHISTLED when he answered the door and saw Becca. She wore some sort of silky, black maternity dress with a halter top. Her bare shoulders invited his touch, as did the deep vee of the neckline.

"You look beautiful."

"Thank you." She smiled, but seemed distracted.

"Is anything wrong?"

"No, not at all. Are you ready?"

"Yes. Do you want me to drive?"

"No, I promised to be the hostess tonight and that includes driving. I read an article online about dating etiquette and I want to do my fair share."

He held up his hands. "I'm not arguing."

"Good." Her smile was more relaxed. She linked her arm through his. "I'm looking forward to a nice dinner and adult conversation without any of the tricky undercurrents at home."

"Jim and Irene still giving you a hard time?"

"They're thawing a little, but it's still uncomfortable. I wish they wouldn't move. It'll change everything and I don't think I can handle that right now."

"You've had enough change for a while, haven't you?"

"Yes."

They headed out to the car and Rick entered the passenger side of Becca's minivan.

It seemed odd not to be driving, but he was determined not to push the issue. He'd decided he had been overly sensitive about the whole mix-up at the doctor's office.

Besides, there was a way to make sure it wasn't simply a misconception that he was Becca's husband and the father of her baby. He could actually become her husband and by default the father of her child. Maybe not biologically, but the only father the baby would ever know.

The more he thought about the idea, the more he liked it. And it would probably help defuse Jim and Irene's animosity, too, once they knew he was doing the right thing by Becca. Marriage would prove how he felt about her and that he wasn't trying to take advantage.

"What're you smiling about?" Becca asked.

"Just thinking."

"About what?"

"Not now. Maybe I'll tell you later."

"That sounds awfully mysterious."

He grinned. "Yes, it does."

"Now you've got me curious."

"Good. I like to keep you wondering." He wanted to touch her, but thought better of it while she was driving. "You know, the way you look in that dress, *I* might take advantage of *you* in the parking lot."

"Remember, we're supposed to be cooling the whole sexual thing."

"Hey, you asked me to dinner. You said it was a date. I guess maybe I chose not to understand the guidelines very well. Or hoped you might change your mind."

Becca sighed. "How could you understand when I'm so unclear myself about what I want?"

"I was hoping you might want me."

"Oh, I do want you, Rick. That's the problem. Way too much for my own good. Maybe we could just be a little more…circumspect."

"You mean sneak around?"

Becca pulled into the parking lot of a steak house tucked away from the house. She put the gearshift in Park and shut off the engine.

"You say that like it's a bad thing," she joked. But there was a trace of sadness in her eyes.

"While there is a certain appeal to sneaking

around—" he cupped her neck with his hand and kissed her deeply "—I have another solution."

Becca touched his cheek, her fingers feather soft. "What's that?"

"Marry me."

"What?"

"Marry me."

She withdrew her hand, glancing out the side window.

He waited, holding his breath.

Her eyes were suspiciously bright when she turned her head to meet his gaze. "Do you love me, Rick?"

"Of course. I wouldn't have asked you to marry me otherwise."

But her question made him realize love hadn't been his biggest consideration in asking. Trying to ensure a place in her life had been higher on the list.

"Usually a guy tells a woman he loves her long before he asks her to marry him."

"I know I haven't told you before, but I do love you. I want to be with you, raise this child together. Be a family."

She kissed him on the lips, a sweet, sad kiss full of regret. "I'm not ready for marriage yet, Rick. And I have to wonder if you'd be asking me if I weren't pregnant."

Rick hesitated.

"See? You wouldn't have to think about it if you were sure."

"But—"

She pressed her finger against his lips. "No, you don't need to say anything. I'm touched and flattered that you asked."

A vague sense of relief told him she might be right. But disappointment soon followed. Especially when he recalled that Becca hadn't told him she loved him. Maybe that was the real reason for her refusal.

Dinner turned out to be a stilted, uncomfortable affair. When they reached Becca's house, Rick was more than happy to get into his SUV and head home.

BECCA WAS RELIEVED that Maya and Aaron were engrossed in a movie when she let herself in the front door. It seemed Jim and Irene had already retired for the night. And David wouldn't be home for hours.

She went up to her room and reclined on the chaise lounge Gabe had bought her for Christmas.

Squeezing her eyes shut, she wished he were here to advise her. But then again, if he were here, she wouldn't be in this predicament.

They'd be eagerly anticipating the birth of their child.

A part of her wanted to jump at Rick's marriage offer. She cared deeply for him and he represented the stability she'd felt sorely lacking since Gabe's death. But she wanted more than stability. She wanted the kind of love she'd shared for so many years with Gabe. Maybe she was fooling herself. Maybe that kind of love only came along once in a lifetime. Rick's proposal had lacked the passion of a man who wanted to spend the rest of his life with her. It had sounded more like a man trying to do the right thing, whatever that was.

So Becca had made the monumental decision tonight to go it alone. Because the whole relationship thing with Rick was driving her crazy. Things would be clearer after the baby was born in little more than two months.

After the baby was born.

But that wasn't what she'd told him. She'd made some indefinite, vague reference to continuing as they had been. Becca realized she'd been doing some seriously skewed thinking. And what if he really did love her and his proposal had just come across wrong?

Becca wanted to smack her forehead. After twenty-three years of marriage, hadn't she learned *anything* about communication?

She almost smiled at her mistake. In her relationship with Rick, everything was new—including misunderstandings. Maybe he truly didn't love her as much as she wanted, but she had to find out.

Slipping on her shoes, she went downstairs. She grabbed her keys and told Maya she would be back in a couple hours.

Driving as if on autopilot, Becca wondered if Rick would understand. This whole relationship thing was scary and exciting and, hopefully, totally worth it.

Rick answered the door almost immediately. "Becca, is something wrong?"

"No, everything's fine. Well, not fine, but can we talk? I feel like our conversation earlier was all wrong."

"Sure. Come on in."

She followed him into his house, noting the comfortable furniture and lack of feminine touches.

"Can I get you something to drink? Bottled water, fruit juice?"

"No. I need to say this while I've still got the courage."

He led her to the couch, where they sat down. "What's going on?"

"When you asked me to marry you, I made

a rash decision and didn't explain myself." She chuckled hollowly. "I guess I've forgotten how to communicate."

"I'm listening."

She twisted the band on her right hand, where it felt out of place but oddly okay. It was her wedding band. She extended her hand to show him the difference. "I changed this on my way to your front door. To show that I'm making room in my life for you. See, I made your proposal an either/or kind of thing. Either we marry now or we don't get married at all. But then I realized you never put those restrictions on it. I did."

"I'd like to marry you before the baby's born. That way I could feel as if I'm the father, even if I'm not."

"That's what I thought. I should have explained that I would feel as if I were dishonoring Gabe if I remarried before the baby was born. My husband at the time of the birth will be the legal father. I feel like I would be erasing Gabe from even the smallest contribution to this child's life. Denying this final gift to me. It would be the last straw with Jim and Irene, too."

Rick hesitated. "I don't agree, but I guess I can understand how you see it that way. My proposal didn't come out very well because I didn't plan ahead. I *do* love you."

"I wasn't sure if you were asking me because you loved me or because you're a good guy and thought it would be the right thing to do." She grasped his hands. "I love you, Rick. I don't know where it will lead, but I'd like to find out. I just don't think marriage right away is a good idea."

Rick brushed her cheek with his fingers. "You love me? You're making room for me to be a bigger part of your life?"

"Yes."

"So we're absolutely clear, I'd want to marry you even if you weren't pregnant." He kissed her, long and lingeringly. "And I'll try not to be jealous of Gabe, even though it means my life is on hold."

"I just don't see any other way."

Rick did. But he didn't dare voice his suggestion. Because if it came to choosing between him and Gabe, he suspected Gabe might win.

Still, he couldn't seem to stop himself from trying. "Becca, I have no problem raising your child as my own. I'm even willing to be engaged to be engaged, if that is less intimidating than an actual engagement. But will you at least consider discreetly getting a paternity test after the baby's born so we know for sure?"

"And what then?"

"We know where we stand. Would you acknowledge the child as mine if it turned out to be?"

Becca glanced away.

"Becca?"

"Part of me wants to agree, since I'm so positive this child is Gabe's. But I don't want to lie to you. I'm not sure if I can do what you've asked of me."

"So you would ask me to lie, if the child turned out to be mine?" He couldn't quite keep the bitterness out of his voice. "You'd want me to keep on pretending I'm raising another man's child?"

Becca stiffened. "Why are you doing this? The baby is Gabe's child and all the what-ifs in the world aren't going to change that. It's cruel to even be having this discussion."

Rick grasped her shoulders, turning her to face him. "I don't mean to hurt you. But we can't hide from the truth, whatever it turns out to be."

Becca's heart constricted at the choice he'd given her. "I love you, Rick. But a paternity test will only hurt the other people I love. I can't do it."

"Irene and Jim?"

"And my children. This baby is a tie to their father. A wonderful miracle. If we find out differently, how will they feel? That I betrayed their father? Betrayed them? I have no idea if it will affect their ability to bond with their new brother or sister."

He brushed the hair from her face. "Those are all valid concerns… But I have to wonder if you're afraid that the baby's paternity might become common knowledge and people might think that you slipped, that you're less than perfect."

"That's a horrible thing to say."

"I'm not trying to hurt you, Bec. I'm trying to make you face things you're not willing to face. Sure, you might be able to bury what we did for a while, deny it ever happened. But you'll always wonder. And the baby may pick up on your emotions. Do you want that?"

"Of course not. You're making this harder than it has to be."

"Hard as it is, I think maybe it's time to bring the truth out into the light. It might shock a few people, but the people who matter will stand by you. And I'll be at the front of the line."

Becca's heart ached at what he was asking. She brushed away the tears on her face. "How can I tell Irene and Jim this might not be their biological grandchild?"

"I don't know, Bec. But I do know you'll do it in the kindest manner possible."

It felt as if the room was closing in.

"No, I can't." She jumped up. "You're asking too much. I came here hoping we could compromise, find a way for both of us to be happy. But you won't rest until you've destroyed the last good thing to happen with Gabe. And I won't allow you to do it."

He rose, grasping her arms. "Becca, wait—"

"No." She wrenched from his grasp. "Let me go."

The abrupt movement made her stomach tighten.

"Are you okay?"

"Yes, I'm fine." Becca glanced at her watch while she calmly walked past him to the door.

She breathed a sigh of relief when she climbed into the minivan. But her relief was short-lived. Her abdomen tightened again.

Becca rubbed her stomach. "No, baby, it's not time yet," she whispered.

CHAPTER TWENTY-FOUR

BECCA DROVE HERSELF straight to the emergency room, where she sat and waited, timing the contractions. They were at irregular intervals, thank goodness.

Retrieving her cell phone, she called home. It seemed Maya took forever to answer.

"Hi, it's Mom. I'm having some contractions so I came by the emergency room. I didn't want you to worry if I was late. You can go ahead and go to bed."

"It's too early for the baby to come, isn't it?"

"I'm hoping it's false labor. If it is, they can probably stop the contractions and I can come home."

"But if it isn't…"

"We just won't think of that right now." Because that would mean the baby was preterm and might face health challenges. And she was in no way ready to bring a baby home. She didn't even have a crib. "Just be sure to take care of your brother until I get home."

"Sure, Mom. I love you."

"I love you, too, honey."

Becca clicked off her phone as a woman in scrubs called her name. She was taken to an examining room, where the nurse took her vital signs.

"We're going to hook you up to a fetal monitor and make sure everything is fine."

After the monitor was attached, the nurse said, "The doctor will be with you shortly."

By shortly, she must have meant sometime before the next decade. But Becca felt reassured by the fact that the baby's heartbeat was being monitored.

Another nurse started an IV. A tech person came and drew blood and asked for a urine specimen.

But Becca was still waiting for the doctor an hour later when Maya came through the privacy curtain, followed by Irene and Jim.

"You didn't need to come. They'll probably just monitor the baby and then release me."

Irene grasped her hand. "Of course we needed to come. We've acted like a couple of old fools. Haven't we, Jim?"

Jim shifted. "Yes, we have."

"Forgive us, dear?" Irene asked.

Becca blinked back tears, realizing how much she'd missed their previous closeness. "Of course. But there's nothing to forgive. We're in uncharted territory here and there aren't any written guidelines. We'll just grope our way along."

"The important part is that you and the baby are safe. We left David in charge at home."

The doctor entered and Irene shooed Jim and Maya to the waiting room.

"I'm Dr. Richards," she introduced herself. "I called Dr. Barker and she'd like us to continue monitoring you without resorting to medication if possible. We're hoping you're just a little dehydrated and fluids will stop the contractions. Especially since they're irregular."

Becca nodded.

But the contractions didn't stop. They started coming closer together and at regular intervals, so the medication was administered via her IV.

When the nurse checked on her later, Becca said, "That must've done the trick. The contractions have stopped."

"We'll keep you under observation for a little while longer to make sure. Then you can go home."

"That's wonderful." Becca leaned back against the pillows, closing her eyes in relief.

A few moments later, she felt someone cradle her hand. She opened her eyes.

"Rick."

"I'm here, Bec. I got here as soon as I heard."

She was so glad to see him. It felt like a lifetime since she'd seen him earlier in the evening. But then she remembered there were too many things between them to resolve. She struggled to sit up.

"Just rest."

"How'd you find out?"

"David called to let me know he wouldn't be able to play racquetball tomorrow. Said he was in charge of Aaron while you were at the hospital."

"That was very…responsible of him."

"Yeah, and a little uncharacteristic. Maybe he just thought I should know."

Becca swallowed hard. "This doesn't change anything."

He sat on the bed, squeezing her hand. "Yes, it does. I was scared I might lose you or the baby. That would destroy me…I love both of you with my whole heart."

"I love you, too. I'm so glad you're here." She kissed his knuckles.

"What're we going to do, Bec? I love you so

much it hurts, but I can't just roll over and play dead about…the paternity thing."

"I know you can't. Could we simply set it aside for later? All I want is a healthy baby. I don't want to worry about anything else."

"Yeah, we'll just agree to disagree right now. Will that work?"

Becca nodded, her eyes filling with tears. He brushed the moisture from her cheek.

Then the curtain parted and Irene and Maya came in.

They glanced at Rick.

"I'm glad you're here," Irene said. "Becca needs you." She went to him and placed her hand on his shoulder. "I'm sorry for being upset about the two of you dating. I only want you to be happy."

Becca's eyes grew moist again as she watched Rick clasp Irene's hand and squeeze. His voice was unsteady when he said, "It means a lot to hear you say that."

"Especially since we're engaged to be engaged," Becca announced.

Rick raised an eyebrow. "We are?"

"Yes, we are. I'm accepting your earlier offer. If it's still available, that is." Becca held her breath and waited.

"Of course it is. I love you, Bec."

"Congratulations, dear." Irene kissed her on the cheek. "Now, we're going to take Maya home and give you two some time to talk. I trust Rick will give you a ride when you're released?"

"Absolutely."

"Goodbye, dear."

"Goodbye, Mom." Maya kissed her mother and they left.

"Engaged to be engaged, huh? I didn't expect you to go for that, but I'll take what I can get. Do I buy you a ring?"

Becca smiled. "Only if you want to."

"Oh, I want to all right." Rick leaned forward and kissed her tenderly.

Becca was so very glad he'd decided to be a part of her life no matter what. She absolutely knew everything would be all right.

BY MONDAY AFTERNOON, Becca was sure she would go stark raving mad. The doctor had recommended a week of rest following her premature-labor scare. Though she hadn't been sent to Siberia—total bed rest—it sure felt like it.

She pounced on the handset when the phone rang.

"Hey, it's me. How's it going?"

"Hi, Rick, I'm *so* glad to hear from you."

"Wow, I love your enthusiasm, but I was there just last night."

"Yes, and I appreciate so much that you brought me pizza and movies. I guess I'm kind of at loose ends. I'm not used to being inactive like this. My life is pretty full from the moment I get up in the morning till the moment I go to bed. Especially since Gabe died."

"It'll be good for you to take things slower. Better for the baby, too."

Becca sighed, rubbing below her breastbone. "I hope so. This baby seems to be pushing on my ribs."

"Sounds…uncomfortable."

"You have no idea."

He chuckled, a warm, rich sound that made her relax.

"How're things going at the agency?" she asked.

"Good. Busy. We miss having you here, but we'll get by. Do you mind if David puts in a few more hours this week?"

"No. He's not taking summer school, so he can work all the hours he wants. Within reason, of course."

"He said pretty much the same thing. With

the qualifier that Friday and Saturday nights are out. New girlfriend, I think."

"He hasn't mentioned anyone, but things have been so chaotic here lately."

"Her birthday's this weekend. He's making some sort of digital slide show for her. I saw him take something out of the glove box of his truck the night of the accident and I was afraid it might be something contraband. Turns out it was a digital memory card with the photos he intended to use. It's such a different world than when we were young."

"Yes, it is."

Becca frowned. She felt as if her children were slipping away. David and Maya both had social lives they tried to keep separate from her and it hurt. Where she'd once been the center of their universe, now she was banished to the sidelines.

"I better get back to work. I'll stop by tonight with takeout—maybe even orange chicken if you promise to take a nap this afternoon."

"For orange chicken, I promise."

"Good. I'll bring enough for Irene and Jim, too."

"I'll let them know. See you tonight."

Leaning back in her easy chair, Becca sighed. Enforced rest meant she had entirely too much time to think. If David was making thoughtful gifts for his girlfriend, then it must mean things were serious.

Loss swept over her. First, she'd lost Gabe so suddenly. Now her children were drifting away.

The baby kicked, reminding her that she would be the center of someone else's universe for many years to come. And she still had a few more years to enjoy Aaron before he asserted his independence.

Her family was changing, no doubt about it. Soon, the baby would expand the dimensions. And after that, Rick.

Becca smiled at the thought. Rick represented the stability she'd felt lacking in her life since Gabe died, but more than that, she enjoyed spending time with him and couldn't wait to start their life together. She could easily see them parenting the younger two children and being terrific grandparents when the time came. And she would become a stepmother to Rick's daughter. Her family was growing, rather than disintegrating. It was a wonderfully reassuring thought.

After a short nap, Becca picked up the newsletter from Aaron's school. They were having a silent auction to benefit the boy with leukemia. There was a picture of the child, bald from chemotherapy.

Becca's heart contracted for his mother. What a terrible tragedy. Losing Gabe had been so wrenching, she could only imagine losing a child.

The baby kicked, then did a move that felt like somersaults. "You'll be fine, baby," she said as she caressed a knee or elbow with her fingertips. And she knew it was the truth.

WHEN RICK ARRIVED at Becca's house, he had to set down sacks of takeout to ring the bell. Aaron answered, grabbed a couple bags and told him to come in.

He entered and placed the food on the counter.

"Mom, food's here," Aaron called.

Rick grinned. "I can see where I rate."

Aaron shrugged, mystified.

Becca wandered in from the great room, yawning. "I guess I must've fallen asleep."

He went to her and gave her a hug. "There's something different."

"I think the baby changed position today. Finally, I feel like I can breathe."

Rick placed his hand on her belly, delighted when the baby kicked his hand. "Just make sure you don't get in too big of a hurry to come out, kid."

"No contractions today. And I'm feeling better since I've had a couple of catnaps."

He kissed her, but not nearly as passionately as he would have wished.

When he drew away, she told Aaron, "Go tell everyone the food is here. Don't forget Grandma and Grandpa."

Then she took his hand and led him toward the great room. "I need to talk to you for a minute."

His heart dropped.

She drew him to the far side of the room, touching his face with her fingertips.

Uh-oh. This was going to be bad.

"I've been thinking a lot about us, the baby, how I want our lives to be. I haven't been fair to you and I intend to change that."

Really bad.

"I've changed my mind. And I want your permission to tell everyone the truth."

"The truth?"

"About the baby."

"Becca, are you sure you—"

"It scares me to death. But it's something I have to do as long as I know you're okay with it."

This was what Rick wanted, but he had to make sure Becca realized what she stood to lose.

She could very well lose the love of her in-laws and the respect of her children. He knew how much both meant to her.

"I'm not the one with the risks here," he said quietly.

"I've had a lot of time to think the past couple of days. I need to do this for the baby, for all of us. I love you so much. But the secret would eventually drive a wedge between us, threatening our chances of having a happy, healthy family together. Besides, I want our child to have the best of everything, and the best medical care involves doctors who have access to a full medical history."

"Has something happened?"

"One of the boys in school with Aaron has leukemia and needs a bone marrow transplant. It got me thinking how unreasonably selfish I'm being by refusing to find out the truth. I love you and my family too much to allow secrets to poison our lives. I fully understand what I'm risking and I'm prepared to accept the consequences."

"If you're sure this is what you want, I'll support you one hundred percent."

"I'm positive." Her lips trembled. "Scared but positive. I love you, Rick."

In that moment, he accepted that she loved him in the only way that mattered. The fully committed, forever kind of love. There were no second bests.

"I love you, Becca."

BECCA BARELY TOUCHED a bite of her food. Her stomach churned, she felt shaky with nerves.

This was big. Really big.

Fear threatened to overwhelm her.

But she resolutely kept it at bay. She had to tell the truth and hope for the best from everyone. And hope they loved her enough not to judge.

Irene and Jim had treated Rick well at dinner and that gave her hope. Maybe things would turn out all right.

"Well, I'm going out to the shop," Jim said. "Thanks for providing dinner, Rick."

"Wait," Becca called. "Before you go, I'd like everyone to meet up in the great room. I have something I want to tell you."

She glanced at Rick.

He nodded in support. She knew he'd be there for her no matter what, and that knowledge strengthened her.

"What's going on, Mom?" Maya asked.

"You'll know in a moment."

She headed for the great room and stood in front of the television set, the focal point of the room.

The people she loved most in the world filed in and sat down.

Becca cleared her throat. "I'm not sure how to begin."

Irene's eyes clouded with concern. "Is it the baby? Is something wrong?"

"It *is* the baby, but not in the way you mean. As far as I know, everything is fine. I've been wrestling with whether it would be more hurtful for me to tell the truth or keep quiet. After reading more about Brandon Jakes's bone marrow transplant, I decided we all need to know the truth."

"What is it, Mom?" Maya asked.

"I want all of you to know how much I love you. *Nothing* will ever change that. After I tell you my news, I'd like you all to keep in mind Aaron's age. I will answer detailed questions in private if necessary."

David frowned. "You're scaring us, Mom. Out with it."

"Okay. I'm not proud of the timing, but here it is. After everyone left for the movies the night of your father's wake, I kind of lost it. I was overwhelmed by my grief. Rick brought in some paperwork he'd promised and found me that way. In my grief, I reached out to him." Becca raised her chin. "We made love that night."

Irene's gasp echoed Maya's.

"That fact doesn't take away from the love I felt for your dad...for Gabe. I loved him deeply and with my whole heart. But in these past few months I've fallen deeply in love with Rick."

She focused on Rick, holding his gaze. "Rick, I love you with my whole heart. I'll always treasure what I shared with Gabe. I also know you and I will build many new memories for us to treasure."

"I love you, too," Rick murmured.

Everyone started to talk at once.

Becca raised her hand. "Irene and Jim, I love you like you're my own parents. I realize what an incredibly difficult position this puts you in and that's one of the reasons I've hesitated to say anything. I won't go into the details, but the child I carry is most likely Gabe's. But there is a small chance it isn't. I hope you will continue to be as closely involved with this child as with your other grandchildren no matter how this turns out. To me, you are the baby's grandparents."

Rick's parents had passed away years ago, so there would only be two sets of grandparents to consider.

Irene's voice trembled when she said, "You've given us a lot to think about. Please give us time to assimilate all this."

"Absolutely. Rick has asked me to marry him and I originally said I wanted to wait until after the baby was born for certain legal reasons. I've since decided I'd like to marry him as soon as he's willing."

Rick grinned.

"After the baby is born, we'll have a paternity test. The results won't change a bit of my love for this child and I hope it won't change yours, either. For medical reasons, we may someday need that information at a moment's notice."

"What's a paternity test?" Aaron asked.

"You and I can discuss that a little later in your room if you'd like, honey."

He nodded.

"That's it for my announcement."

Her family was unusually quiet as they filed out of the room.

Rick opened his arms and she walked into them.

"You are a tremendously brave woman. I'm so lucky to have you."

She reached up and touched his face. "No, *I'm* the lucky one. Nobody tarred and feathered me, so that's a good sign."

"Time will tell if they can accept the truth. But we'll handle whatever comes our way. Together."

She smiled, her eyes sparkling. "Does that

mean we'll both explain a paternity test to Aaron?"

Rick laughed and pulled her close. He kissed her, a gesture full of passion and promise. "If that's what it takes, then we'll talk to him together. We're a team now."

EPILOGUE

RICK WATCHED the church fill on the morning of the christening. Theirs was truly a blended family. Becca's children and Rick's daughter sat in the front row. Becca's father and step-mother sat with her brother, Royce, and his family. Rick's ex-wife and her husband sat behind Kayla.

The ceremony seemed to take forever, though he knew it was only a few minutes. Finally, the godparents were asked to step forward. Royce and Katy McIntyre rose.

Rick held his breath.

Jim and Irene Smith also rose and stepped forward. Their voices were firm as they agreed to look after the spiritual needs of the infant.

A swell of gratitude overcame him. His precious daughter was fortunate to have so many people who loved her.

He slid his arm around Becca's waist and squeezed.

She smiled up at him, his wife, his partner, his friend and lover.

They were a family.

"Gabrielle Irene Smith-Jensen," the pastor intoned as he christened their daughter.

Baby Gabby didn't fuss. She simply watched him with wide eyes.

Rick's heart skipped a beat, as it often did when he saw his new daughter. Because she was, miraculously, both the daughter of his heart and his biological daughter. But he would have loved her just as fiercely if she hadn't been his blood, because she was part of the beautiful woman he loved so much.

AFTER MAKING SURE there was still plenty of food and drink for their guests, Becca managed to find a semiquiet moment in the kitchen to stop and count her blessings. It was a difficult task because her blessings were constantly increasing.

She watched Irene pick up Gabrielle and coo to her while Becca's parents and Jim stood close, waiting their turn to spoil the baby. The children milled around and mingled with the rest of the guests. Maya's and Kayla's friends were fascinated with the baby, Aaron's ignored her and David's kept their distance.

Finally, her gaze rested on Rick, the man who was the center of her universe. He caught her staring and winked, his smile full of promise.

Becca's brother came over and bumped her with his shoulder. "Hey, sis, how're things going?"

Becca beamed at him. "This is the best day ever."

* * * * *

Enjoy a sneak preview of
MATCHMAKING WITH A MISSION
by B.J. Daniels, part of the
WHITEHORSE, MONTANA *miniseries.*
Available from Harlequin Intrigue
in April 2008.

Nate Dempsey has returned to Whitehorse to uncover the truth about his past…

Nate sensed someone watching the house and looked out in surprise to see a woman astride a paint horse just on the other side of the fence. He quickly stepped back from the filthy second-floor window, although he doubted she could have seen him. Only a little of the June sun pierced the dirty glass to glow on the dust-coated floor at his feet as he waited a few heart-beats before he looked out again.

The place was so isolated he hadn't expected to see another soul. Like the front yard, the dirt road was waist-high with weeds. When he'd broken the lock on the back door, he'd had to kick aside a pile of rotten leaves that had blown in from last fall.

As he sneaked a look, he saw that she was

still there, staring at the house in a way that unnerved him. He shielded his eyes from the glare of the sun off the dirty window and studied her, taking in her head of long blond hair that feathered out in the breeze from under her Western straw hat.

She wore a tan canvas jacket, jeans and boots. But it was the way she sat astride the brown-and-white horse that nudged the memory.

He felt a chill as he realized he'd seen her before. In that very spot. She'd been just a kid then. A kid on a pretty paint horse. Not this one—the markings were different. Anyway, it couldn't have been the same horse, considering the last time he had seen her was more than twenty years ago. That horse would be dead by now.

His mind argued it probably wasn't even the same girl. But he knew better. It was the way she sat on the horse, so at home in a saddle and secure in her world on the other side of that fence.

To the boy he'd been, she and her horse had represented freedom, a freedom he'd known he would never have—even after he escaped this house.

Nate saw her shift in the saddle, and for a moment he feared she planned to dismount and come toward the house. With Ellis Harper in his grave, there would be little to keep her away.

To his relief, she reined her horse around and rode back the way she'd come.

As he watched her ride away, he thought about the way she'd stared at the house—today and years ago. While the smartest thing she could do was to stay clear of this house, he had a feeling she'd be back.

Finding out her name should prove easy, since he figured she must live close by. As for her interest in Harper House… He would just have to make sure it didn't become a problem.

* * * * *

Be sure to look for
MATCHMAKING WITH A MISSION
and other suspenseful
Harlequin Intrigue stories,
available in April wherever books are sold.

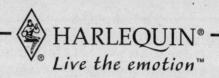

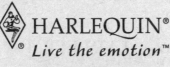

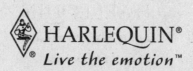

HARLEQUIN®
INTRIGUE®

BREATHTAKING ROMANTIC SUSPENSE

Shared dangers and passions lead to electrifying
romance and heart-stopping suspense!

Every month, you'll meet six new heroes
who are guaranteed to make your spine tingle
and your pulse pound. With them you'll enter
into the exciting world of Harlequin Intrigue—
where your life is on the line
and so is your heart!

THAT'S INTRIGUE—
ROMANTIC SUSPENSE
AT ITS BEST!

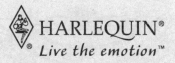

Harlequin® Historical
Historical Romantic Adventure!

*Imagine a time of chivalrous
knights and unconventional ladies,
roguish rakes and impetuous
heiresses, rugged cowboys
and spirited frontierswomen—
these rich and vivid tales will
capture your imagination!*

*Harlequin Historical . . .
they're too good to miss!*

HHDIR06